Shades Of Lust

Sexy Stories Collection

VOLUME 14

17 EROTIC SHORT STORIES

BLAINE TELLER

Shades Of Lust/ Blaine Teller. -- 1st ed.
Xplicit Press, an imprint of TLM Media LLC

ISBN-13: 978-1-62327-545-7
ISBN-10: 1-62327-545-8
eISBN: 978-1-62327-595-2

Printed in the United States of America

CONTENTS

CONTENTS

1 HIS LOVE

Jessica made her rounds with a duster, cleaning all of the guitars and keyboards. It had been over an hour since anyone had come into the music store; all was silent save for the classic rock quietly pouring from the store speakers. A coworker had called in sick, so Jess was stuck working late until the night shift showed up.

The chime on the door jingled and Jess turned to greet the guy who came in. Then she saw who it was and resumed dusting. It just *had* to be that skinny, goatee-bearing college kid who came in often but rarely bought anything.

He leaned on a counter behind Jess and watched her work, shamelessly eyeing her ass. She ignored him for a long time, then eventually, creeped out by his presence, turned to face him.

"What do you want, Andrew?"

"Easy, hellcat, I just came to keep you company. I saw you working late, so I thought I'd offer to buy you dinner after your shift."

"Thanks, but I work on a morning shift tomorrow. After work, I'm just going home and pass out."

"Sad. They let you work too hard out here. If you keep pushing that gorgeous body, you'll be nothing but bones."

"Maybe, but the pay is good."

"You deserve better than being the assistant manager of an all-night guitar shop. Come and be my dedicated groupie. I'll share my wealth."

"Wealth? Are you implying that that band of yours is going to go somewhere?"

"Give it time, doll. People are just intimidated by our sound; once they get used to us, we'll be the biggest thing in the world."

"You do heavy metal covers of '30s swing music. I don't even know how that's possible!"

"Swing metal is going to catch on, just you watch!"

Jess rolled her eyes. "Whatever, Andy. I've got things to do before the night shift gets here. If you want to hang around and stare at me, feel free - though it would be nice if you bought something every once in a while."

"I actually need some guitar strings. I'll get them before you clock out."

"Fine."

Things started to get busy just before the end of Jessica's shift. She was eager to get home, and sighed in relief when she stepped through the door of her small townhouse. She ensured the door was locked behind her, then dropped her purse on a coffee table and left her keys on top of it. It had been a long day; all the shapely brunette could think about was getting some sleep before her morning shift.

Jessica lived alone but sometimes felt like she was being watched. It was creepy but ignorable. She still lived in the house she'd grown up in, having bought it herself some years ago instead of moving out. Her mother moved to Florida with a new boyfriend shortly after Jess bought it; her previous husband, Jessica's stepfather, died when Jess was only ten years old. They had been close before he died, but she could remember little of him.

Stepping into her bedroom, Jess kicked her shoes off and hurriedly stripped clean of her work uniform. Her socks and bra fell into the clothes pile as well, leaving her dressed in only a pair of plain white panties. She pulled on a white camisole, feeling the fabric caress her stiff nipples.

After turning the lights off, Jessica crawled into bed and pulled a thin sheet over her half-naked body. One hand immediately slid down to her crotch; the other grasped at her boob. She vigorously stroked herself through her clothes, intending to get off as quickly as possible. She felt like she was being watched, but she tried to ignore it and focus on what she was doing.

It wasn't long before Jess was panting and bucking her hips. Her talented fingers rubbed her nipples and clit simultaneously, using the fabric as a masturbatory aid. Within a few minutes, she shuddered and let out a long moan. Satisfied, the young woman relaxed. Letting out a happy sigh, she slid her arms under her pillow. It took only seconds for her to drift off to sleep.

A few hours later, Jessica's sheet slid off of the bed. A pair of invisible hands slid up her thighs, then lifted her camisole until her breasts were exposed. The unseen pervert caressed and squeezed the sleeping woman's sensitive tits. His fingers delicately pinched and twisted her stiffening nipples.

Jess stirred in her sleep, slowly waking from her slumber. Moonlight streamed through the window, illuminating the room fairly well. Even in the moonlight, however, Jessica still couldn't see who was touching her. The sensation of fingers on her nipples was distinct and unmistakable, but no one was there. Her hands soon found a man's chest just above her. She could feel him.

"What's going on? Why can't I see you?"

The teasing continued with no indication of stopping. Jessica reasoned that invisibility isn't possible and that she must be dreaming. She decided just to go along for the ride. The unseen stranger released the young woman's nipples and ripped her panties off. She could feel a thick cock grinding against her tiny slit. Nothing wider than her own slim fingers had ever been inside.

"I think you might be too big for me. My little pussy can't handle that!"

Unhindered, the invisible man continued to grind. Once Jessica began to get moist, the thick tip nudged her folds apart. Jess threw her head back and screamed when the girth surged inside, forcing her tight muff to stretch wide. Her juicy pink flower squeezed her lover's shaft tightly.

The big cock went deep - it didn't stop until the head wedged against Jessica's cervix. She screamed again and pushed hard against the unseen stranger. Invisible hips started to gyrate, pounding Jessica's poor little pussy hard and fast. She yelped every time her mysterious lover buried himself in her tightness.

Jess caught sight of the mirror on the opposite wall. She could see her hips floating above the bed and her formerly tight pussy gaping open.

In time, she got used to his girth and her screams dulled into grunts. She dug her fingers into the sheets and clenched tight. Her squeezing forced him to push even harder to keep up the same pace, which increased the pleasure for both of them.

In time, the invisible man thrust deep and held himself there. Jess could feel the wet warmth deep inside her, and she sighed softly. After a moment, he pulled out and rested his still-hard dick against her thoroughly used pussy. The moonlight made their mixed fluids glisten, and Jess could see the outline of a large penis in the juice.

"That was intense! Can you do that again?" The slimy cock slid down until the tip prodded against her puckered anus.

"You want to fuck me there? All right, I guess. Just be gentle, okay?"

The invisible man answered with a short hard thrust. Jess screamed, feeling her virgin ass spread wide open around the head of his cock. With another hard thrust, he buried the remainder of his length in Jessica's rectum. He went far too deep for comfort, making her insides cramp. After savoring her tightness for a few seconds, he began to thrust his long cock in and out of her at a brutal pace.

Jessica writhed on the bed and screamed. Her bottom reflexively tried to push him out, but couldn't even slow him down. Semen oozed out of her pussy and ran down her taint. It added to the wetness on the big invisible cock but did little to lessen her discomfort.

Heavy balls slapped Jess with each savage thrust, filling the room with lewd sounds. She screamed hoarsely, not able to stop screaming even if she wanted to. When her ass loosened up a little, her lover fucked her even faster.

The unseen man didn't take his time sodomizing Jessica and soon pulled out of her tight rump. Thick ropes of pearly white seed shot all over her belly. Invisible fingers played with the cum, shaping it into letters on her tummy. Jess watched the words form; he was writing upside down so she could read it. Once he'd finished, the cum was smeared into a very clear "daddy loves you."

Jessica looked up at the seemingly empty space between her legs.

"Dad? How can...." An abrupt thrust into her ass derailed her train of thought and made her scream again. "Not so rough, you dirty old man. You're hurting me!"

Ignoring her pleas, the ghost of Jessica's stepfather jackhammered her ass, intent on cumming again. After a few minutes, he pulled out and rolled Jessica onto her belly. Jess saw the mattress dip down under his hands on either side of her, then felt his throbbing member return to her body's warm embrace.

"You've been here the whole time, haven't you? Seeing me naked, watching me sleep. You even peep in on me masturbating, don't you? Is that why you're doing this?"

The ghost answered only by slapping her ass.

"You're such a pervert! What would mom say if she knew you were butt-fucking your own stepdaughter?" The ghost silenced her by stuffing two fingers in her mouth. One was the same finger he'd used to write on her, and it still had a hint of salty cum on it. Jessica obediently sucked her stepfather's fingers. In time, the rhythmic slap of hips against Jessica's rump came to an end. Her stepfather's ghost gave one last deep thrust and came inside her. He ground against her for a few seconds, then pulled out. She felt his weight shift on the bed as he lay down next to her. Strong, invisible arms wrapped around Jess and pulled her close.

Jessica melted into his warm embrace. He rubbed her back just as he'd done when she was little and he was still alive. The nostalgia made tears well up in her eyes.

"I've missed you, Daddy."

The ghost held Jess close and stroked her long after she'd fallen asleep. He didn't need rest and so continued his loving caresses all through the night. Jessica slept more peacefully than she had in years, feeling cozy and cared for. Her dreams were filled with a distorted mash-up of memories, combining the events of last night with her memories of his appearance.

The next morning, Jessica awoke in a haze. Her hand swung out to smack the snooze button on her alarm. While sitting up, she noticed that her camisole had ridden up above her breasts and her panties had somehow come off in the night. She remembered having a very intense sex dream, but couldn't remember what it was about. As the fog cleared from her mind, she realized just how sore her lower body was – her butt in particular. To her surprise, she found crusty, dry cum on her skin. Then she saw the writing on her tummy. It was faded but still somewhat legible.

While staring at the faded message, Jess felt a pair of arms wrap around her. She jumped but quickly calmed down as the memories came back fully. Jess twisted around and hugged her ghostly stepfather, wrapping her arms around what appeared to be just empty air. He held her and stroked her back for a few minutes, then grabbed her ass and ground his invisible wood between her legs. Jess tried to push him away.

"Hey, no! I have to get ready for work!" To her surprise, the ghost released her.

"We'll play more later when I get home. Just go easy on me tonight. I'm still sore." Jess grabbed some clean clothes and then turned to face the bed before leaving the room.

"You can watch me shower if you want. I get the feeling you're going to whether I give permission or not, so I might as well."

2 HIS GIRL
HIS LOVE PART 2

After a few months of prodding, Jessica had finally caved to Andrew's advances and agreed to go on a date with him. Despite how annoying she had found him in general, they actually hit it off surprisingly well. Their successful first date was followed by another, and then another. He was a surprisingly funny and charming guy, even if he was also completely ridiculous.

The couple's third date was proceeding as well as usual. Andrew had taken Jessica for a walk on the pier, followed by dinner at an upscale restaurant. Jess actually felt a bit underdressed in her lime-green tank top and white denim miniskirt. Andrew's dark slacks and blazer seemed a bit less silly now. Though self-conscious, she took some comfort in the fact that no one was staring.

"How can you afford to bring me to a

place like this?"

Andrew grinned. "My band did a cover of Benny Goodman's 'Sing Sing Sing' that got a lot of attention. It nudged people towards looking into our other songs. MP3 singles and album downloads started selling like hotcakes. At this rate, we might not have to self-publish our next release."

Jess wore an incredulous expression. "Brasshead albums are selling? I can't believe you're actually making money doing swing metal."

"You don't have to believe in me, but you'd be a fool to doubt the power of metal."

"Apparently so. Wow, I underestimated you guys. Well, congratulations. I'm happy that you found success."

"Thanks, Jess." Andrew was silent for a moment, then smiled and began speaking again. "You know, there's this tradition concerning third dates."

"Are you asking me to have sex with you?"

Andrew hiked a brow. "Ever done it with a rock star?"

Jessica blushed. "No, I can't say that I have."

"Tonight's your chance. You can brag that you took Brasshead's lead guitarist to bed."

"I don't know how my stepdad would feel about that."

"I thought you said you had your own place? Either way, he doesn't have to know. I won't tell if you don't."

"He'll know, trust me."

"How so?"

"Do you believe in ghosts, Andrew?"

"That's kind of a random question."

"Not really, no. You'll see when we get back to my place."

"You mean you'll do it?"

Jessica grinned. "How often does a girl get the chance to take a real, live rock star to bed?"

Dinner passed by in a blur. The young couple could barely keep their hands off of each other during the drive to Jess's place. Jessica and Andrew didn't even wait until they reached her bedroom before they started pulling each other's clothes off. They'd both shed their shirts soon after entering the house, and Andrew was trying to unhook Jessica's bra mid-kiss as they made their way awkwardly down the hall. The lacy black undergarment fell to the floor just as they came to the bedroom door. Andrew caressed Jessica's tits while she reached back to turn the knob.

They didn't break their passionate kiss until the topless brunette hottie fell back onto her bed. Her stiff, pink nipples stood erect in the cool air. Jessica kicked her shoes off and wiggled out of her skirt as her skinny, brown-haired boyfriend took his pants off. Soon they were both clad in only underwear and socks. She could see a nicely sized bulge in his shorts, and he eyed the crease of her panties. Andrew climbed into bed with Jess and they resumed their passionate kiss. While his tongue probed her mouth, his hand slid down the front of her panties to stroke her slit with two fingertips.

She put her hand in his boxers and squeezed his half-mast cock, offering a moan of approval without breaking lip lock. He became hard at her touch, just as she grew moist at his. After a bit of teasing, Andrew wedged his fingers into Jessica's drooling mound. Both young adults were already quite horny. The stroking and fingering just further increased their need. After a few seconds, Andrew pulled his digits out of Jessica's slick passage and peeled her panties off. Jess lifted her shapely legs to help him remove her underwear and then tugged down the waistband of his boxers to reveal his throbbing cock.

Andrew stood and removed his shorts completely, leaving them both in nothing but their socks. He got on top of Jess, ready to sink his length into her glistening snatch. Just before their genitals made contact, an unseen force shoved Andrew out of the way. Jessica's pussy spread wide open around nothing with a quiet, squishy noise. She arched her back and moaned hotly.

"What the hell?"

"Sorry Andy, I guess Daddy wants to go first."

"What do you mean, Daddy?"

"He...ooh, right there! He died when I was very young. But he never really left me. Things started getting physical last year. He's an excellent lover." Andrew vascillated between disbelief and disgust for a few moments, but the sight of Jessica's bouncing breasts and the sound of her blissful moans convinced him to just enjoy the show. He moved so that he could see her pussy, spread wide open around a ghostly penis that was apparently quite thick. Jessica's clear pussy juice coated her stepfather's dick, and her boyfriend could just faintly see the outline of it when he pulled back. Jessica wrapped her legs around her stepfather's waist, bucking her hips up to meet his thrusts. She couldn't help but smile when she saw Andrew stroking himself. She was afraid he'd run away, but he was quite fascinated with the situation.

Jess had developed a taste for rough sex and was greatly enjoying her stepfather's brutal pounding. The ghost's thrusts came hard and fast, rocking Jess's petite frame. He was determined to claim his daughter before this other male could enter. Before long, Jess arched her back and cried out. Her toes curled, and a gush of hot fluids washed over the ghostly cock. Her stepfather wasn't far behind, pressing deep and blowing a big wad of cream into her.

The sight of spunk dribbling out of Jessica's open pussy sent Andrew over the edge. He laid a white stripe across her thigh.

A little landed on her stepdad and hung there, as if it was floating in midair, but the ghost didn't seem to care. After a brief rest, the ghost pulled out of Jessica. He lifted her up off of the bed and turned her around. She could feel his chest against her back. The tip of his spooky penis poked her ass and then pressed inside. She gave him an appreciative squeeze and moaned when he went deeper. The ghost held Jessica by her thighs, leaving her legs spread wide open and her pussy easily accessible. Semen dripped from her stretched pink cunt.

Andrew stared – eyes wide open, mouth agape, and penis hard.

"I think Daddy is inviting you to join, unless you'd rather just watch?" Andrew continued to gawk for a moment, finally moving between Jessica's glistening legs. He guided his rod into her sloppy muffin and thrust hard. She clenched around both males with a moan. Andrew could feel each of the ghost's brutal thrusts into Jess. He tried to match the other man's pace and adjusted his rhythm so that he thrust in as the ghost pulled out, and vice versa. Jessica could do nothing but lie there and moan. Both of her holes were packed full of hot cocks, and she had a pelvis slapping her from either side. Andrew's thrusts drained out her stepfather's cum, forming a sticky mess all over both of their crotches. Wet slaps accentuated each of Andrew's pounding fucks.

A cock in each hole had Jess feeling fuller than ever before. She writhed in her stepfather's grasp, moaning and panting in sheer ecstasy. Despite her efforts to make the feeling last, she couldn't resist her swiftly approaching orgasm. Jess screamed, clenched tight around the thick meat inside of her, and shuddered. Andrew felt her slippery snatch become even wetter.

The ghost was the next to cum. He crammed his cock deep into his daughter's ass and held it there, depositing another big load of his sticky ghost cream. Andrew sped up his thrusts and finished soon after, adding his own load to the white mess already in Jessica's muff. Andrew pulled out of Jess and moved back. Her stepfather pulled out of her as well and sat her down on the bed. She flexed both holes, clenching up tight to hold in as much cum as she could. Andrew felt hands on his shoulders and then screamed when a thick cock pressed into his ass. Jessica laughed.

"Don't fight it. He's not gentle, but you'll get used to him." Jess watched her boyfriend get fucked with a gleeful smile on her face. After a couple of minutes, the ghost pushed Andrew onto all fours and grabbed onto his hips. Andrew tried to follow Jessica's advice and relax, but the painful thrusts had him clenching reflexively. Andrew gritted his teeth and shut his eyes tight. Jess patted him softly on the cheek and he opened his eyes to see that she'd moved a little closer.

Her pussy was right in front of his face now. He obediently dipped his tongue into her, tasting the combination of her sweet flavor with the salty emissions of two guys.

Each inward thrust pushed Andrew forward, and he reflexively rocked back when the ghost pulled out.

Despite the pain, he was starting to enjoy the perverse feeling. One of the ghost's hands moved from his hip to grab his cock, adding a little extra stimulation to the sodomy. As he got more turned on, the tongue lashings he gave Jessica became more intense. It wasn't long before Jessica's ghostly stepfather hit his peak a third time. The feel of hot, sticky cum flooding his sore ass pushed Andrew right over the edge as well. He moaned loudly into Jessica's pussy and came all over the bed. The tongue work kept up until Jess came, just seconds later. Her fluids rushed out to be eagerly licked up by her boyfriend. The ghost pulled out of Andrew's rump and flopped down on the bed. He pulled Andrew and Jessica close to him, one on either side. The two of them cuddled up to him and smiled at each other.

"Jess, I think I'm bisexual."

Jessica giggled. "Dad's just that good."

"So, since I've been officially welcomed into the family, I guess that means we have his approval to keep seeing each other?"

"I would say so. I doubt he would have allowed this three-way to happen if he didn't like you."

"Good, I'd hate to think I gave up my ass for nothing." The two lovers shared a laugh and then got cozy against the ghostly body between them. He stroked both of their backs while the two of them caressed his chest.

In time, Andrew and Jessica drifted off. Andrew and Jessica continued their relationship, though they never had sex without her stepfather joining in. The happy trio explored many different positions and configurations for three-way sex. Sometimes Jess even took charge with a strap-on.

In time, anal sex became more than just a kinky turn-on for Andrew. He came to find it genuinely pleasurable and welcomed Jessica's toys or her stepfather's cock inside him. Within a few months of his first night with Jess, Andrew moved in with her. The three-way necrophilia became even more frequent with Andrew living in the house.

After just six weeks of living together, Andrew and Jessica got married. It was a small ceremony attended by Andrew's family, Jessica's mother, and a few of their friends. Andrew's band, Brasshead, played at the wedding with a stand-in guitarist.

3 SHADES OF HIS
HIS LOVE PART 3

Jessica enjoyed being the wife of a rock star, but the nights spent apart were an unfortunate side effect. Between practices, recording sessions, public appearances, and tours, Jessica rarely saw Andrew. Andrew's band, Brasshead, was doing surprisingly well with its bizarre swing-metal music. She was happy for his success, but didn't get to see much of him while the band was so active.

Not that she was completely alone in his absence. The house in which they lived was haunted by the ghost of her step-father. Her stepdad had been looking after her from beyond the grave for a longer time than she could know. Things had gotten physical a few years ago, though. Her relationship with him had forever changed for the better.

Every night, she was ravished by her ghostly step-father. They indulged in three-ways when Andrew was there, but he would have her whether or not her husband could join them. Jess never felt bad about cheating on her husband. The relationship with her step-father had begun before her first date with Andrew, and she felt confident that he had an army of groupies waiting to sate him after every show. Though the ghost was incorporeal, he always left a load of very real spunk inside her—often more than once each night.

That had become something of a problem. Jessica's period was late. Though she doubted the possibility of pregnancy, she bought a test just in case. The test indicated positive. She stood in the bathroom, staring at the indicator in disbelief. Andrew most likely wasn't the father; the timing was all wrong. There was one other possibility, though it seemed impossible and certainly wasn't wanted.

With a sigh, Jess tossed the test into the trash. There would be time to make sense of things after a hot shower. She turned on the water and adjusted it to her liking. Then, she peeled off her panties and moved the shower curtain just enough to enter the tub. Hot water rained down upon her bare flesh, soothing the agitated young woman.

Jess didn't touch the soap. She just spent a short while relaxing, caressing herself under the warm rain. The shower curtain moved, coaxing a startled gasp from Jessica. Suddenly, a human silhouette formed in the shower stream. With water running onto him, Jessica's step-father was the most visible he'd been since his untimely death.

"Good morning, Dad. I think you should know something." Jess paused for a reaction. The ghost just stared at her mutely. "I'm pregnant, and I think you're the father."

The ghost hugged Jessica tightly, holding her nude body against his invisible figure. His lips pressed against hers, and his tongue slithered into her mouth. It was the first time they'd kissed in such a way, and Jess found it a bit odd. He was standing right in front of her, with his tongue in her mouth, and she still couldn't see him.

Invisible hands roamed all over Jessica's body, caressing and groping her wet flesh. She broke the kiss when she felt his erection brush her thigh. The groping became more intense, reflecting the perverted ghost's one-track mind. His hips rolled, grinding his stiff cock against her slick, wet flesh.

"You dirty old man. Don't you ever think about anything else?"

He answered by lifting Jess up and pressing her back against the wall. She wrapped her arms around his neck and her legs around his waist. His invisible girth surged into her glistening honeypot with a single push. Jess cried out at the sudden entry, but his short, swift humps had her moaning in just seconds. Her pussy flexed around his exquisitely thick member in a rhythm that perfectly complemented his.

Jessica's soft moans echoed within the small bathroom. The ghost's powerful hips jerked that fat cock back and forth inside his step-daughter's tight snatch. Jessica had been a virgin when her stepfather first took her, but playing with him regularly had taught her to love sex – the rougher, the better. She bucked her hips to eagerly meet every thrust, moaning as she did so.

The ghost squeezed his step-daughter's rump tightly, digging his fingers into her tender flesh. Jess cried out and clenched his cock tighter. Her step-father compensated for the extra grip by humping even faster. The young woman's slick snatch eagerly swallowed the ghost's invisible manhood. Her body accepted every powerful thrust.

Jessica's taut figure writhed and shuddered. Her sopping wet muff rippled around the ghost's rock-hard girth, massaging his tool. His thrusts grew longer and rougher as the two of them got more worked up. His crotch pummeled hers in swift, forceful strokes. Each meeting of their wet bodies produced an audible slap that echoed within the tile-lined chamber.

The sating of her step-father's otherworldly lusts brought Jessica great pleasure. Her body quivered against his in coital bliss. It didn't take long for the young woman to reach orgasm. With a scream and a splash of nectar, Jessica had her first climax of the day. Her pussy flexed erratically around the broad intruder.

The ghost didn't even slow his thrusts during his step-daughter's climax. Her tight clenching forced him to thrust even harder to keep up the same pace. The increased intensity earned a soft scream from her with every thrust. Each rough push extended her orgasm just a little, overwhelming her with rapture.

When Jess recovered from her climax, she resumed the tight clench of her pussy on her dad's member. Her step-father renewed his efforts, increasing the pleasure for both of them. The ghost's thick organ sent waves of ecstasy crashing through Jessica's body. The young woman's skilled muscle control and enthusiasm ensured her step-father shared in this wondrous pleasure.

It didn't take Jessica long to reach another breathtaking climax. This time, her step-father came with her. Just as she gushed her sweet love onto him, his spooky penis erupted into her pussy. Thick spurts of supernatural spunk jetted into Jessica's muffin. She timed her flexes to milk him dry, giving his rod a firm squeeze between shots of cum.

The spirit ground his hips against his step-daughter for a few minutes and then pulled out of her. Excess semen drooled out of her well-used pussy, dribbling down onto the floor of the tub. The pooled sexual fluids were quickly rinsed away by the running water.

Jess lowered her shaky legs to the floor and removed her arms from her step-father's neck. Before she could even fully stand, the ghost grabbed her by the shoulders and spun her around. The spirit pressed Jess firmly against the wall and shoved his cock into her pert bottom. His slippery, invisible girth forced her anus open and slid inside easily.

Jess cried out and flexed tightly. The next few thrusts were slow and easy, but the ghost sped up the very instant Jessica relaxed. His strong hands pinned her to the wall, keeping her tits mashed against the wet tile. Each thrust moved her slightly, filling the bathroom with the squeaky sounds of wet flesh sliding on smooth tile.

The ghost was anything but gentle with his step-daughter's bottom. Not that he was ever really gentle during sex, anyway. His enthusiasm left Jess with an uncomfortable cramping for a few minutes. She was used to roughness in the rear, though. Once her body adjusted itself after the ghost's entry, things felt a lot smoother.

Jessica's hips swayed from side to side, wiggling her ass while her step-father fucked it. Her motion made every thrust hit her at a new angle. The ghost responded to the new motion by humping even faster. His invisible hips spanked her, reddening her buttocks. The wet slaps grew ever louder as the ghost increased his pace a little at a time. Her booty clenched tighter around his organ, and he thrust harder to maintain his speed.

Sooner than expected, Jess found herself shuddering and screaming. The exquisitely brutal sodomy had brought her over the edge without so much as a single clit stroke.

Her juices ran down her thighs, mingling with the hot water spewing forth from the shower head.

The savage ravishing of Jessica's clenching bottom continued for several more minutes. Her tight rear entrance eroded the ghost's willpower swiftly, though. He soon wedged himself inside as deeply as possible and filled his step-daughter with sticky love. Each blast of cum sent a shiver through Jessica's young body.

Jess remained smashed against the wall, panting. The ghost held her there for several more minutes. After a brief rest, he pulled his softening shaft free of her buns and released her from the wall. She suddenly felt very empty without his thickness filling her rump, though she could still feel the warmth of his cum deep inside.

While Jessica caught her breath, her step-father lathered up a loofah with soap. He gently scrubbed his step-daughter's body. Jess sighed happily and moved as he needed her to, allowing him to scrub all of her naked form. His free hand caressed and teased her bare flesh. Those naughty fingers found their way to all sorts of places, getting Jess worked up all over again.

The ghost's hand suddenly left Jess's body. He made more suds with the bar soap, this time covering his dick. Jess looked over her shoulder, able to get an accurate look at how big he was for the first time ever. She didn't get to stare at his soapy dick for long, though. The ghost thrust his sudsy penis into Jessica's pussy, coaxing an adorable yelp from her lips.

Jessica shuddered, accepting each rough thrust into her needy snatch. Her step-father ravished her hard and fast, sending a mixture of pussy juice and soap froth to the shower floor. Jess screamed and writhed in the ghost's strong grasp. He continued to scrub her with one hand and grope her with the other. The frantic humping didn't affect his pace in the slightest.

When the soap suds were nearly gone from the ghost's cock, he pulled out of his step-daughter's muffin. Jess heaved a disappointed sigh, but wasn't made to wait long. Her step-father re-soaped his penis and then buried himself in her tight ass. Jessica screamed and rocked her hips back, accepting every inch of her ghostly dad into her greedy backside.

The ghost pummeled Jessica's bottom much faster than before. Jess gritted her teeth and groaned. She felt like her ass was on fire. The sound of his hips smacking her wet butt drowned out everything else; she could scarcely hear herself think. Thoroughly warmed up, Jess felt little more than pleasure from the brutal sodomy. Each rapid drive into her rump pushed her just a smidgen closer to the peak.

Despite her best efforts, Jessica couldn't hold back and make it last. She cried out and clenched tightly around her father, writhing in ecstasy. Her orgasmic convulsions brought him crashing over the edge right along with her. The ghost pulled his erection free of Jessica's rump and shot rope after rope of sticky spunk onto her back. The salty spirit spunk ran down the young woman's back, mingling with the hot shower water and making even more of a mess.

Jessica leaned against the wall, panting heavily. Her step-father resumed scrubbing her, now in a significantly less sexual manner. The rough surface of the loofah traveled all over her naked flesh, cleaning every bit of spunk and sweat from her. He was very gentle with her tender places, washing by hand the skin that was too sensitive to be scrubbed by the loofah.

Once Jess was clean, the ghost placed the loofah in the soap dish. He planted a tender kiss on his step-daughter's lips and vanished. She rinsed herself in the hot water, then turned the spigot off and got out to dry herself. Jess donned some comfortable pajamas and took care of what housework was left for the day.

Jessica had the day off work and decided to spend it relaxing around the house. The bulk of her time was dedicated to curling up on the couch with her Kindle and a good e-book. Her step-father came to see her several times throughout the day, ravishing her once more each time. His attentions were often centered on her backside, but she didn't mind a bit.

They maintained their sexual relationship throughout the first two trimesters of Jessica's pregnancy. The ghost took her very gently when she started to show, a slightly alarming change of pace from his usual jackhammering. He got only a little rough when taking her from behind, and he never thrust hard into her pussy. She didn't allow him to enter her during the third trimester or the six weeks after her daughter was born. He respected her wishes, but the instant she offered herself to him again, he went back to his usual self.

Jess had a healthy baby girl. She looked much like her mother but had some traits from her late father. Despite Andrew having no part in her creation, friends and family still insisted that she looked just like him. No one would ever know the truth of Emma's conception or the relationship Jessica had with her step-father.

4 QUEEN OF THE FOREST

Humans had long known The Great Southern Forest to be inhabited by the devious elves and vicious goblins. Neither species had ever been fond of humans, but few in the human kingdoms know that they once fought each other just as fiercely. With the elves in the west end of the forest and the goblins in the east, the space in between was often a battlefield.

For decades, each species of forest dweller fought fiercely for control of the other's lands. The goblins had the advantage of superior metalwork, but the elves had many talented archers and trap makers. The racial feud was a long and bloody war of attrition with many losses on both sides.

A truce was eventually declared, but tensions remained high. Morion, the king of the elves, began sending his only son, Darrian, to goblin lands as an emissary amongst a company of his strongest and most trusted guards. The peace talks went well, but some suggested that Prince Darrian and Queen Haruko had a more than diplomatic interest in each other.

One evening, Darrian came to the goblin queen's palace to meet with her again. He was tall, lithe, and fair-haired; typical for an elf. What muscle tone he had was concentrated in his arms, a result of his archery training. A trio of guards in shiny ceremonial armor followed close behind him, armed with halberds.

Haruko was a head shorter than Darrian, which made her of above-average height for a goblin. Her skin was green, and her hair was dirty blonde. Rather than the traditional royal garb, she'd chosen to wear something a fair bit more scandalous this day. Her violet gown was low-cut in the front, displaying her cleavage. One side was slit from hem to waist, leaving her legs almost fully exposed.

Darrian entered the throne room. He and Haruko exchanged flirtatious glances while a pack of heavily armored goblins eyed the elf prince and his bodyguards warily.

"So, the handsome elf has returned to me."

"How could I stay away, Queen Haruko?"

Haruko smiled. "I believe we have spoken of everything that can be discussed in a throne room. Prince Darrian, would you join me in my personal chambers? In private I believe we could better discuss how to deepen the bond between our peoples."

"Yes, I believe a private discussion would

be most appropriate. Some things are not meant for the eyes and ears of guardsmen." Darrian turned to face his bodyguards. "Stay here until I return."

Haruko stood from her throne, then walked to Darrian and took his hand in hers. She led him up a set of stairs to a heavy oaken door. Beyond lay a large room dominated by a huge bed with silken sheets. Three smaller doors lined one wall. A red-haired goblin servant stood near the door, awaiting commands.

"Shina, you are to prepare a bath for us in the morning," Haruko said. "You have the rest of the evening to yourself."

"Thank you, Your Majesty."

"Darrian and I are not to be disturbed tonight. You may watch if you wish."

Shina blushed deeply. "I would do no such thing, Your Majesty. I swear it."

Haruko grinned wickedly. "Do not lie to me, Shina. I know you like to peek."

Shina's blush deepened. "I apologize, but I must take my leave. Enjoy your evening Queen Haruko, Prince Darrian." Shina hurried to one of the doors on the wall and disappeared into her quarters. Darrian and Haruko watched with bemused expressions.

"Your servant is a voyeur?"

"She would never admit to such, but there are complaints from guards, other servants, and even some of the nobles. She has a fascination with men masturbating, but has also been caught watching couples several times."

"Let's give her a good show - I would hate

to disappoint the poor girl."

"I could not agree more."

Haruko stepped out of her velvet slippers, then pulled off her gown in one swift motion. She wore nothing underneath, fully exposing her nude form to Darrian. Her nipples were dark green, the same as her lips. The goblin queen's shapely body was completely hairless save for the dirty blonde mane atop her head and a matching thatch of thick bush above her crotch.

Darrian didn't hesitate to strip out of his clothing as well, though it took quite a bit longer for the elf to get naked. His body also lacked hair, saved for his head and groin, though his bush was smaller than hers. The goblin queen's eyes zeroed in on the elf's semi-erect penis. She watched him stroke it to full hardness for her.

The elven organ was long and slim compared to a typical goblin tool: about seven inches in length but around 3/4 an inch in girth. The bulbous head hid beneath a thin foreskin. A ring of spines surrounded the base; another was located just behind the head. Haruko grew a bit nervous, staring at the spiked cock while Darrian climbed into bed with her.

The couple kissed passionately, entangling their tongues. Darrian's hands found Haruko's breasts and delicately teased her stiff nipples. Haruko's hands drifted down to touch the elf's hard cock. She felt his penis barbs graze her skin while she stroked him. She felt at once scared and excited, not knowing what sort of sensations his thorns would give.

Haruko broke the kiss and moved back slightly. She bent forward and took Darrian's member into her mouth. Her tongue slithered into his foreskin to tease the sensitive glans within. She felt his barbs prickle against her lips while she suckled him. One of her hands stroked his long shaft while she tasted the tip.

Darrian slid his hand along Haruko's back until he reached her rump. He gave her pert bottom a squeeze, then felt around for her slit. Haruko groaned when Darrian found her sensitive vulva. His middle finger stroked back and forth across her lips. When she grew moist for him, he slid his finger inside.

Haruko bobbed her head swiftly along Darrian's rod. His spines tickled the inside of her mouth with every little motion. The elf's finger pumped swiftly in and out of her, soon joined by a second. Haruko moaned loudly around Darrian's meat, then slid her mouth off. She lied back and opened her legs, proudly displaying her slippery green snatch to the elf.

"Take me, prince! I can wait no longer."

Darrian didn't hesitate to mount Haruko. He guided his erection into her hot folds, the couple moaned together. The elven shaft vanished into Haruko's pussy little by little. She could feel his barbs drag along her inner walls all the way in, sending a pleasant tickle through her pussy.

The goblin groaned quietly when Darrian bottomed out inside her. She was able to handle his full length quite comfortably. The lovers spent a few moments caressing each other and enjoying the mutual feeling.

With some hesitation, Darrian slowly pulled back. Haruko moaned the entire time, her back arching and her hips bucking. The elf's spines dragged along her inner surface all the way, sending waves of ecstasy through her lower body.

Darrian made slow, tender love to the goblin queen. His hips rolled in a smooth, steady rhythm. The feel of his barbs spoiled Haruko; she knew she wouldn't be able to get off on a smooth goblin cock ever again.

The unexpected stimulation drove Haruko to an orgasm rather quickly. She dug her nails into Darrian's back and cried out. Her pussy squeezed tight around him, and a burst of moisture washed over his groin.

Once the goblin queen had climaxed, Darrian sped up significantly. Haruko screamed and held onto the elf for dear life while he jackhammered away at her slippery green pussy. The feel of his cock spikes was even more intense with the added speed.

Haruko writhed and bucked, driven to climax after climax by Darrian's barbed tool. His spines tickled her just right, as though his cock were specifically crafted for her pleasure. The lewd sounds of sex grew louder and louder with every wet orgasm Haruko had.

Darrian held back for as long as he could, intent to leave a good first impression of elven sex firmly implanted in Haruko's mind. In time, his willpower gave out. After a few more short, swift thrusts, he buried himself deep inside her and came. He shot several thick ropes of hot elven cum into the goblin queen's tightness.

The couple held each other and shivered, riding out a shared afterglow. Their lips met in another fiery kiss, and their hands roamed each other's nude bodies. After a while, Darrian pulled himself free of the queen's embrace.

The elf began to leave the bed, but Haruko grabbed him by the shoulders. "Don't you wish to stay the night with me?"

"I'd not want to impose."

"Please, I insist."

"Very well then, my sweet Haruko."

Darrian curled up next to Haruko, the couple entangling their arms in a sweaty, naked cuddle. With some mutual caressing, the two of them drifted into a deep sleep together.

When Darrian awoke the next morning, Haruko was gone. Shina stood nearby, staring at the floor. The elven prince stood, hiding his shame with his hands.

"Where has Haruko gone?"

"She is bathing and would like for you to join her. Through this door, right here."

Darrian opened the door without hesitation and went inside. The interior of the room was a pretentiously decorated marble chamber, dominated by a large tub in the center. The tub was filled with hot water, with a thin layer of bubbles across the top. Steam rose from the surface.

Haruko was in the bath already, eyeing her lover lasciviously. "Good morning prince. Please, join me."

Darrian lowered himself into the hot water, sitting directly across from Haruko. The tub was small, but able to accommodate the both of them comfortably enough. All of the skin-on-skin contact and warmth had Darrian growing a bit excited. Soon, the tip of his elven shaft proudly emerged from the water.

"Goodness, is that for me?"

"For you and you alone, my beloved Haruko."

The goblin queen wrapped her fingers around Darrian's member, just below the surface of the water, and began to stroke. The motions of her hand were slow and sent little waves through the tub. Darrian leaned back and opened his legs as much as he could in the tub, allowing Haruko to do as she pleased.

The goblin caressed and fondled along the elf's tool, exploring him fully with her small, slender fingers. After a short while of teasing, her strokes became swifter and more determined. Darrian let out a quiet groan and closed his eyes, content to just enjoy the ride.

As Haruko grew more excited, her hand moved with increasing swiftness. The water splashed each time her fist broke the surface, stroking the elf fully now. Darrian's length throbbed strongly in her grasp, encouraging her even further. She used her thumb to tease the underside of his head on the upward apex of each stroke, furthering his pleasure.

Finally, the elf came. With a loud groan, Darrian tossed his head back and ejaculated. Streams of sticky white love splattered all over Haruko's face and breasts. The goblin giggled and collected a dollop of cream on one of her fingertips, then sucked it clean.

"My my, are all elves so tasteful?"

"I should think not, our species would go extinct were elven women to prefer using their mouths."

Haruko laughed, then gave Darrian's cock a squeeze. "I hope that you are not sated already? I had hoped to repeat our performance from last night."

"Your touch has but stoked my appetite."

"And mine as well."

Haruko stood, then straddled Darrian. Her lower body was covered in suds. Without a hint of hesitation, she dropped herself onto her lover. She took his full length with a splash and a moan, gripping the spiked elven spear tightly in her warmth.

The goblin bounced excitedly on the elf's lap, making waves in the tub. His hands roamed her body, sliding down her back to squeeze her ass and then caressing back up again.

Unbeknownst to either of them, the door was open just a crack. Shina peeped in, getting a good view of the show. She could hear the splashing and the moans. She could see the slippery, naked bodies grinding together in carnal bliss.

The queen's servant lifted her skirt and put a hand between her legs. She tickled herself until she could stand no more teasing, then buried a trio of fingers in her drooling muff. Biting her lip in an attempt to silence herself, Shina pumped her digits in and out of her body at the pace of the queen's bouncing. She pictured herself on Darrian, pretended she was the one being speared on his length.

Haruko leaned in and kissed Darrian fiercely. They moaned into each other's mouths, but the kiss broke when the elf slapped his goblin lover's ass. She sped up her motions, riding her elven mate even harder. The waves grew taller, soapy water splashed over the edges of the tub. Darrian and Haruko's voices rose in volume with the intense sex.

It didn't take long for Darrian's barbed tool to make Haruko cum. Her orgasmic clenching, her angelic moans, her slippery breasts sliding across his chest, and the feel of her supple ass in his hands—it all combined to bring Darrian right over the edge with her. He bucked his hips upward, burying himself as deep in the goblin queen as he possibly could, and let out a sharp grunt. A thick wad of his hot spunk burst into Haruko's eager depths.

Shina didn't take much longer, excitedly stroking her most sensitive places while the bathing couple caught their breath. She dug her nails into the doorway and fought hard to stop herself from moaning out loud. Wet warmth washed over her hand, and her entire body shivered.

"Shina! Bring a mop!"

The servant jumped, blushing darkly. She stepped back from the door and turned her head, trying to make it sound like she was not standing directly in front of the door. "At once, my queen!"

Shina made her way to her supply closet to retrieve a simple mop and a metal pail. She entered the bathroom and tried to pretend she wasn't looking. While mopping up the water, she snuck glances at Darrian's smooth chest and Haruko's exposed breasts. The lovers were now resting on opposite ends of the tub again, both looking quite satisfied.

In time, the couple finished cleaning up. They got dressed and shared a final kiss before leaving the royal bedchamber. Haruko returned to her throne, and Darrian gathered his guards. They'd passed the time playing dice and seemed quite annoyed upon Darrian's return.

"Where have you been, my lord? We were about to come looking for you."

"My apologies, guardsman. Queen Haruko and I engaged in some...intense negotiations."

"You negotiated all night?"

"I did not expect to be gone so long, or I would have secured accommodations for you."

Another guard hiked a brow. "You are smiling too broadly to have spent the night discussing politics. I think there is something you're not telling us."

"Do not overstep your bounds, guardsman. What transpired between me and Haruko last night was our private business. I say we were negotiating, and that is that."

Darrian and Haruko shared a knowing glance; then, the goblin queen spoke. "Your men are surely tired; I am sorry for making them wait all night. Had I known our talks would last as they did, I would have arranged for them to rest in the servant's quarters. Please, allow me to prepare a carriage. Your guards should not be made to march sleepless in a time of peace."

"That is quite considerate of you, Queen Haruko. We thank you for your kindness." Darrian nudged one of his bodyguards; the three of them mumbled thanks to the goblin queen.

Darrian and his men returned to elven lands in a wolf-drawn wagon driven by a goblin. The elves were leery of a goblin carriage, but could clearly see their prince as a passenger and did nothing to inhibit the cart's progress. After delivering its passengers, the cart turned and began the journey home.

The peace talks between Darrian and Haruko continued. From that day on, they always took place in Haruko's bedchamber. Rumors abounded, but only in hushed whispers. An interspecies relationship would be quite the scandal for either ruler, but none were so bold as to lob accusations.

Though both races remained highly distrustful of each other, border towns began to integrate little by little. Seen by some as an abomination and others as progress, the image of goblin and elf living side by side served as a clear indicator of the changing times.

5 QUEEN OF THE FOREST II

Long-standing tensions between goblins and elves had eased over time, however slowly. In the years since open fighting had ceased, Prince Darrian of the elves and Queen Haruko of the goblins had urged their peoples for lasting peace. The integration of border towns was a good sign, but cohabited areas tended to be high in violent crime.

The death of King Morion meant Darrian would assume the throne. By elven custom, no elf may rule without marrying. King or queen, the elven heir needed a royal consort before officially taking power. A line of elven noblewomen had begun courting Darrian the moment Morion's health began to fail.

Darrian rejected all of his potential brides. In an act that shocked everyone, he instead openly proposed marriage to Haruko. The goblins had no custom requiring their ruler to be married, and so

Haruko had remained single. Interspecies marriage, however, was completely unheard of in either culture.

Haruko's acceptance ballooned the scandal further. Old rumors of Darrian and Haruko's indiscretions resurfaced. Though Darrian and Haruko each insisted the marriage was for political reasons only, few believed them. When the location they'd selected for the wedding was revealed, it was immediately vandalized. A modest mansion for both rulers to live in temporarily was constructed in a border town. That, too, was vandalized.

Under heavy resistance, the elven king and goblin queen continued to plan their wedding. The ceremony was attended by a few nobles of both species. Many family members and associates had been invited, but most refused to show. It was still the first time so many elves and goblins had been in the same room together without fighting.

For the sake of neutrality, Darrian and Haruko were actually married twice—once under elven marriage custom and again under goblin marriage custom. The newlyweds retired to their mansion after the ceremony. Rumors immediately sparked among both species. Each claimed the other was trying to take over the entire forest.

Darrian carried Haruko up a set of wooden stairs. Their home was nicer than any ordinary mansion, but not quite up to the level of luxury either monarch was accustomed to. A proper palace had been planned for the same city. It was to use materials from the existing palaces of both rulers. The palace, however, would take over two decades to build. Their home would suffice until then.

The bedchamber was large by conventional standards and contained a massive canopy bed. Darrian laid his new bride on the sheets and kissed her lips tenderly. They pulled at each other's clothes while their tongues wrestled. Laces and buttons came undone, loosening the ostentatious wedding garb.

The kiss broke and they began hurriedly removing garments. A pile of expensive, exquisitely tailored clothes formed on the floor. Darrian crawled into bed, nude. Haruko joined him, wearing only her stockings. They kissed again, each exploring the other's mouth while their hands roamed each other's naked flesh.

The goblin's touch excited her husband. His barbed, elven cock slowly grew hard for her. She felt him harden against her thigh, but playfully ignored his erection. Her touch graced every part of him that she could reach, except for his manhood.

Darrian was not quite so subtle. His touch gravitated towards his wife's breasts, again and again. Each time he caressed elsewhere, he came back to her tits just seconds later. Her nipples were stiff for his touch. He teased her firm nips delicately, handling them as though they were precious jewels.

Haruko finally gave up on teasing her lover and reached for his cock. She curled her fingers around his girth and squeezed, feeling it throb in her grasp. Darrian moved a hand down to her crotch as well. He stroked her slit, feeling her moisture on his fingers. Satisfied that she was ready, he slid a finger into her tight passage.

The couple moaned in unison, a sound muffled by their ongoing kiss. Darrian easily found his wife's G-spot, something she'd taught him how to do years ago. She broke the kiss to gasp in pleasure, but he quickly brought his lips to hers again. She used her other hand to tease him as well, cupping his balls in one hand and stroking his tumescent shaft with the other.

Minutes later, Haruko broke the kiss and pulled away from Darrian. She sprawled out on the bed, legs open wide. Her puffy, dark green labia glistened with moisture. Darrian planted his face between her legs and enthusiastically tasted her. Haruko arched her back and moaned. The feel of his tongue thrilled her, but she gently pushed him away.

"Take me, my love. I can wait no longer."

Darrian wasted no time in mounting his lover. He pressed his spiked cock into her wet muff and penetrated her slowly. Their lips met and muffled their mutual moaning. Haruko clenched tightly around her husband's hardness. The slow, inward push allowed her to feel every detail of his rod.

Once the elf bottomed out in his goblin mate, he began to pull back. His barbs scraped along her inner walls the whole way out, making her squirm. When only the head remained inside, he thrust into her again. His movements were slow and deliberate. He took his time in making love to her, and it was driving her wild.

Haruko's juicy goblin twat clutched Darrian's barbed elven dick tightly. The tighter she squeezed, the more of an effect his spines had on her. Her body trembled every time he pulled back. She wrapped her arms and legs around him, digging her nails into his back.

Darrian maintained the same slow, tender pace. Haruko drifted through a sea of pleasure, savoring every thrust of his prickly penis. After a while, it became too much for the goblin queen. She broke the lip lock with her lover and let out a wail of pleasure.

It was only after Haruko's orgasm that Darrian sped up. He took her in swift, deep thrusts. She yelped each time he buried himself in her. Every slam extended her orgasm a little. Her clenches and blissful vocalizations helped him topple over the edge with her. The elven king buried himself in Haruko one last time and moaned loudly. His spines flared, and hot seed erupted into her depths.

The lovers lay still for a while, holding one another while they caught their breath. Darrian made sure to pull out before his penis barbs could fully retract, making Haruko shudder. He looked down at her mound with a smile, watching his pearly white virility drool out of her.

"Are you ready to go again, my love?"

"Soon, my sweet." A curious expression crossed Darrian's face. "There is a certain elven custom concerning newlyweds."

"What is it?"

"A newly married couple should engage in anal sex on the night of their wedding."

"Is that really a custom of your people, or did you just make it up?"

"I am the king; I can make new customs if I choose to."

"Is that so? Well, it is a goblin custom that a gentleman should prepare a lady's backside with his tongue before penetrating her."

"Strange how our customs mesh so well together. We may live to see a unified civilization after all."

Haruko laughed and rolled onto her belly. "Be gentle, Darrian. My bottom has never known the touch of a man."

Darrian caressed Haruko's rump, kneading her round cheeks in his hands. He parted her buttocks and delicately traced his tongue around the rim of her anus. Her pucker flexed with each motion of his tongue. The warm, wet feeling made her squirm. It was a bizarre, but not entirely uncomfortable, sensation.

The elf's tongue swirled in slow circles, coating the goblin's sphincter in saliva. She began to relax a little, and he slipped his tongue inside a short distance. He wiggled it for a few seconds, then withdrew and replaced it with a finger. She moaned quietly and clenched tight around his digit. He wormed it deeper, exploring her insides as far as he could.

After a few seconds, Darrian pulled his finger free of Haruko. She sat up on her hands and knees, offering her butt to him. He got behind her and gripped her hips. The tip of his erection wedged between her buns. The elf tilted his head down and spat on his own dick. Then, he nudged Haruko's anus and gently pressed inside.

The goblin groaned, feeling her sphincter part to allow the elf inside. The stretching was mildly uncomfortable, but not as bad as she had expected. She was willing to try this, so long as he was willing to be gentle. Darrian soon found that he could not fit his entire penis in his lover's rear entrance. Her colon made an abrupt right angle after about five inches.

The elf withdrew, scratching the inside of the goblin's ass on the way out. She found his spines to be quite a bit less enjoyable in her butt, though the sensation still wasn't a bad one. He took her very slowly, mindful of the lack of proper lubrication. She dug her fingers into the sheets and tried to relax. Her bottom squeezed and pushed, reflexively trying to push the intruder out.

Haruko moved one hand between her legs to play with her clit. The pleasure helped her distract herself from the odd feeling of a dick in her ass. She began to relax more, allowing Darrian to sodomize her with greater ease. His pace remained slow and steady, giving her plenty of time to get used to it.

The goblin grew more comfortable with the act. She tried to control her clenches. Darrian felt her flexing differently and paused to add a little more saliva to his shaft. Newly spit-lubed, he humped faster. Haruko cried out in surprise, but not pain.

The elf's barbed shaft vanished between the goblin's green ass cheeks again and again. She lowered her upper body onto the bed for more comfort, still holding her ass up in the air. Darrian leaned forward and wrapped his arms around Haruko. He held her tightly against his chest, supporting his lower body with his knees alone. He kissed her neck while thrusting swiftly into her backside.

Haruko panted heavily, letting out quiet moans between breaths. She strummed her clit insistently, soon getting her other hand down there to finger herself as well. The goblin worked herself up enough to climax. She cried out and clenched tight around Darrian's cock and her own fingers.

Darrian followed soon after. He pressed into his wife's rump as deeply as possible and moaned. His spines flared once more, and his twitching cock fired a generous load into her bowels.

The lovers rested in that position for a little while. Haruko could feel her lover's barbs poking against her rectum from all directions. When Darrian's cock began to soften and his spines relaxed, he pulled out. The withdrawal was very slow, making Haruko writhe.

Once he was out, she rolled over and gave him a passionate kiss. He enthusiastically kissed back, holding her tightly. After a few minutes, Darrian broke away and lay down next to Haruko. The newlyweds cuddled and slept, sated for at least a while.

The joint announcement that the two monarchs would combine their power and rule the forest together was met with much resistance from elf and goblin alike. There were threats of secession and even open rebellion. The guards thwarted many assassination attempts. In spite of it all, Darrian and Haruko remained together.

The great southern forest was not unified in a day. Though under joint rule, there was great unrest across the land. Local leaders often disobeyed royal edicts, some less discreetly than others. By the time the palace was finished, though, resistance had faded. Tensions remained, but many of the forest dwellers had come to accept the change in political structure.

The rumor that Queen Haruko had become pregnant was eventually confirmed by the birth of a son. Bearing both goblin and elven traits, Ostrava was declared a living embodiment of the spirit of unity. His birth inspired a wave of interspecies marriages between elves and goblins. Many of the couples had previously kept their relationships secret, for such a thing was still considered scandalous even after so much time.

History would show that the combined wisdom of Darrian and Haruko did much good for both the elves and the goblins. A new army formed, utilizing elven tactics and goblin-made equipment. When the humans invaded their shared lands, it was only through the combined strength of both races that they were driven back. Though opinions on interspecies marriage remained mixed, the last opponents of unification changed their minds with the defeat of the human invaders.

Ostrava grew into an honest and generous prince. His parents did not officially declare him an heir until they were certain he would rule benevolently. In time, Darrian and Haruko grew old and stepped down from the throne, together. King Ostrava was courted by many a woman, goblin and elf alike. It was rumored that he took many of his potential brides to bed before declining their advances. He eventually married another hybrid like himself. King Ostrava and Queen Maryha ruled as the new king and queen of the forest.

6 PROBED

Spring nights have always had a bizarre way of making me horny, I don't know why. Whether it's the warmth, the smells, the colorful wildflowers, the animal hormones in the air, or all of the above; just taking an innocent hike at dusk in early spring has always been enough to get me soaking wet.

One night, I was taking such a hike when the urge began to overtake me. I headed for this nice little clearing I like to use to take care of myself. It was nearby, and provided enough privacy that the people living nearby wouldn't be able to see me from their homes. It wasn't much, just a roughly round patch of grass about ten feet across with no trees or other large flora. I sat with my back against a tree, facing the rest of the clearing. I didn't mind getting my long, brown hair dirty in the tree bark. I intended to skinny dip in the creek afterwards, anyway. I cupped my large breasts, and teased them through my tight tank top. One hand remained on my tit, the other migrated south and slipped down the front of my shorts. I was already nicely worked up from just walking there. Wasting no time, I wedged three of my slender fingers into my tight twat with a low moan. The thought that another hiker, or maybe even some random animal might be watching added a dirty thrill to the act. Eyes closed, I vigorously pounded my wet beaver. My hips bucked, my back arched, and my moans came freely. I felt like I was floating. Then I realized that I really was floating!

I opened my eyes to see a bright green light all around me. Gravity had ceased to exist within the shaft of light. My body floated casually upwards, joined by twigs, seed pods, and various other forest floor debris. I pulled my hand from my shorts and tried to escape, but I couldn't get anywhere.

Eventually, I passed through some open doors on the underside of a flying saucer. The doors slid close behind me, and the beam suddenly cut off. I fell to the floor with a grunt. It wasn't too much of a drop, but I thought I might have bruised my butt. A door on the wall slid open, and three humanoid aliens walked in. They had gray skin, big heads, and large black eyes. They all wore identical silver suits. The aliens bound my hands and feet, and then picked me up. I didn't put up much of a struggle, interested to see what they might want to do with me. I would preserve judgment of these creatures until they did something unsavory.

I was brought to a large room with lots of bizarre looking equipment and hoisted onto an examination table. One of my captors pulled out a curved knife and I panicked a little, but he cut my clothes off without harming me. He next cut my temporary restraints, then he and his comrades shackled my hands to the sides of the table. My feet were shackled into stirrups, holding my legs up in a bent position. I was fully exposed to these aliens, embarrassed and aroused.

"You guys are thorough! This is one of those sex abductions, I hope? I'd rather not have my organs harvested."

None of the three of them answered my question, but the one on my left said something to the other two. In retrospect, it was silly of me to expect them to speak English. One of them brought over some sort of medical-looking machine. Two lengths of insulated wire led from the back of the machine to a pair of suction cups.

"Are you studying humans for something?" Again, none of them said anything I could understand. The suction cups were attached to my nipples. One of the aliens flipped a switch on the machine and the suction cups started to vibrate. I gasped and writhed on the table. The vibration made my sensitive nipples even stiffer than they were before. While distracted, two of my captors wheeled in another machine.

I saw a rubber phallus and took it to be some sort of anal probe, but I had to crane my neck to get a good look. The dildo had a pointed tip and gradually thickened until about the half-way mark, then narrowed down to a slender base. The machine itself was fairly simple and unscientific-looking; a motor, some steel rods, and a controller. It didn't look like a device designed for gathering information.

"You guys aren't scientists at all, are you? You're a bunch of interplanetary perverts! But I actually kind of like where this is going." One of the aliens smeared some lubricant on the dildo, and then lined it up with my asshole. Another manipulated the controls, and the entire six inch toy disappeared in my ass with a single push. I arched my back and gasped, surprised but not hurt. I squeezed around the oddly shaped phallus, loving the thick part in the middle. The toy began to slide in and out of me at a moderate pace. The machine made a soft whirring sound while it sodomized me, just a bit quieter than the buzz of the nipple vibrators.

"You three abducted the right girl, anal is my favorite!" While I reveled in the feeling of mechanical butt sex, the aliens stripped out of their shiny clothing. They were all quite stiff already, and I could see that the dildo in me had been modeled after one of their cocks. A light gray shaft that bulged out in the middle, leading to a pointed, dark gray head.

They had no visible external testicles, but aside from that their anatomy wasn't too different from a human's. One alien took his place between my legs, another in front of my face, the last joined me on the table. My sopping wet pussy was suddenly violated by a thick gray cock; he used all of the patience and consideration his machine had shown me. The alien on top of me spat into my cleavage and squished my tits together around his dick. The alien behind me made me tilt my head back until he could shove his cock in my mouth.

I could feel the cock in my pussy moving at the same rhythm as the dildo in my ass. The alien pushed in just as the machine pulled back, and contrariwise. When the machine sped up, he moved to match the pace. The nipple vibrators ramped up their efforts as well, buzzing more loudly and ravaging my hard nips. That alien cock pounding between my tits was quite a turn on, too. I didn't mind the guy fucking me in the face, but I'd never sucked a cock before and I had no way to tell if I was doing well at it. I definitely put in the effort, sucking hard and stroking him with my tongue while he slapped my face with his pelvis. I gagged a little every time he nudged the back of my throat, but I could handle him. It didn't take long for me to cum like this. I bucked and screamed, but my vocalizations were muffled by a mouthful of dick.

They weren't quite done with me, however. All three aliens sped up their humping, making me writhe and moan on the examination table. Both machines were turned up in their respective settings, flooding my oversensitive body with even more ecstasy. The time passed with a blur, in what felt like minutes I was already cumming again. This time, the aliens were close and came soon after me. The guy in my pussy shot first, going deep and grunting. His organ throbbed hard and filled me with hot spunk. The guy fucking my mouth went next, giving me a big wad of sour slime. Once he pulled out, I spat the purple gunk on the floor. Finally, the guy fucking my tits blew his wad, shooting purple alien jizz all over my chest and neck.

My captors got off of me and shut down the anal probe. I got one last hard thrust, then the toy pulled out of my bottom. I suddenly felt very empty, though the tiny vibrators within the suction cups continued to stimulate my nipples. Two of the aliens began to clean me up, while the third left the room. The gray pervert soon returned, carrying the biggest dildo I have ever seen in my life. It had to be at least 27 inches long, and wickedly curved. The shaft was about three inches across and covered in ridges along the entire length, spaced about an inch apart. The head was a bit thicker than the shaft, and covered in rounded rubber spikes. I couldn't tell if the toy was supposed to resemble a creature from their planet, or if it was just a naughty fantasy.

With the press of a button, the gray dildo

came loose and was set aside. It took two guys to attach the giant dildo; one to hold it and the other to insert a support rod into the socket. One began to lubricate the gigantic toy while another smeared lubricant on my ass. The third just watched while I stared at that huge cock in terror.

"Where the hell do you think that thing's going? That'll kill me!" I struggled against my restraints, but it was no use. There was no escape, though I bruised my wrists and ankles trying. The tip of that ridiculously huge cock touched my anus, I clenched in fear. "Please, no! Don't do this, I'll do anything you want! Wouldn't you rather just fuck me some more? You can't do this to me!"

My protests didn't sway the alien creature, if he even understood them. Holding the controller, he made the machine push the dildo up inside me. I screamed, feeling my anus open wider than ever before. That giant rubber cock slid further and further into my body, moving very slowly. It was soon uncomfortably deep inside me, in addition to being painfully thick. I could see my belly bulge out once it got in so far. I had never realized before how deep I actually am, the toy was able to get further than I would have imagined.

It did, however, hit a wall before I could take the full length. The sensation of having something that far inside me was quite painful, and I screamed again. The alien adjusted the controls and pulled the toy back just an inch. He left it there for a moment, then turned the knob. The toy pulled back until just the head was inside, then drove right back in to the programmed stopping point. They all watched while the probe violated me, slowly but firmly. I could see the obscene bulge in my abdomen every time it went deep. The machine was making me take what had to be 13 inches of rubber phallus with every push. Tears ran down my cheeks. Despite the pain, it was also really turning me on. I'd never taken anything so large or so deep, and now I was being pushed to my limits.

After a while, an orgasm caught me by surprise. I cried out and bucked my hips. Slippery girl cum splashed onto my thighs and lower belly, the warmth made my skin tingle. It had been a long time indeed since I'd been turned on enough to squirt. The pain in my ass hadn't faded, but the pleasure was growing stronger in spite of it - or perhaps because of it. I found myself wondering if I'd ever be able to get off on a regular dildo again.

Finished with their break, the aliens took their places around me. All three of them were rock hard again. I couldn't tell who was in what position, they all looked the same to me. They stuck their cocks in my pussy, my mouth, and between my tits just like last time. My captors didn't bother with a slow start now, they just went at me hard and fast. The nipple vibes rose in power - an empty gesture, for my nipples had gone numb a while ago. The probe sped up as well though, now taking me swiftly. I screamed every time it pushed into me, and my vocalizations made the alien in my mouth moan. It was hard to care about what they were doing with their cocks while the giant probe devastated my ass. I could feel them all having their way with me, but all I could focus on was that enormous dildo. I came again, soaking an alien's crotch in my Earthling fluids. My ejaculation seemed to turn him on, he started fucking me even faster. A load of alien cum shot into my pussy just as I was cumming on him again. The other two followed soon after, filling my mouth and coating my neck respectively. I swallowed the alien cum this time, if only to say that I had. My captors pulled away from me again, but remained close-by. The probe gradually came to a stop, then slowly pulled out of my ass. I could feel my rectum prolapse a little, but I was able to right myself with a few clenches. The nipple buzzers stopped as well, and were removed. "Thanks guys, that was actually kind of fun. We should do this again, after I've recuperated." One of them brought over a hose with a nozzle at the end and put the tip in my mouth. He depressed a button on the side of the nozzle, and a strong-tasting liquid sprayed out. My mouth burned, my eyes watered. I reeled back as much I could. When my lips were free of the nozzle, I spat out the offending fluid.

"This is gin! I'm a recovering alcoholic, you asshole!" Unfazed by my insult, he sprayed some booze on my face, neck, and tits. Afterwards, they unshackled me and allowed me to get off of the table. I couldn't walk right, but they helped me back to the bay where I'd first entered the ship. They left me alone there, and a bright red light filled the room. The doors opened, and I began to slowly drift back to Earth. They weren't putting me back in the woods, though. I could see the streets from up in the sky, and I could tell I was just a couple of blocks from home. I'd never been on this street in particular, though. As I got lower, I realized they were lowering me into someone else's swimming pool. Once I was about five feet above the surface of the water, the beam shut off. I screamed and fell in just as the ship sped away. It was past midnight, the water was pretty cold.

That's how they left me. Naked in a stranger's pool, reeking of sex and alcohol, completely unable to walk straight. No one believed my story, so I eventually just stopped telling it. I never saw those aliens again, but every time I masturbate, I fondly remember the night I got probed.

7 ALIEN AFFECTION

Of all of the science vessels serving the Galactic Alliance, Neo-Ark was by far the largest. Built to house millions of subjects and hundreds of thousands of crew, it was a truly massive starship. That size served a purpose, though. The crew of the Neo-Ark was tasked with the capture and study of animals from distant planets, especially rare or endangered specimens.

We were to collect one of every non-sentient species in Alliance space in order to compare the fauna of various planets on a morphological, physiological, and behavioral level. Needless to say, things had a tendency to get pretty noisy in and near the holding decks.

We were forbidden to let the creatures procreate, as doing so would be a waste of resources. The crew was also forbidden to procreate, a standard part of Alliance Navy policy. Said rule was enforced via segregation, as each Alliance ship could be crewed by only one sex; crews were either male-only or female-only. Being a straight woman on an Alliance science vessel can get frustrating.

That's why I feel for these creatures; they're dealing with the same level of sexual frustration. Just like me, they have to live on a starship far away from home without any hope of getting laid. Even worse, they didn't sign up for it.

My crew mates mocked me for being so in-tune to the feelings of our subjects, but that's why the Alliance offered me this position in the first place. "Exemplary Animal Empathy" is what they called it when the offer came. I was given the choice to either serve out the rest of my bestiality sentence in prison, or as an Alliance scientist working closely with extraterrestrial animals. The choice seemed obvious.

One of the subjects in particular had caught my attention: number 774291 from Berith. The Berithians called their species "klegnar." This klegnar was a hulking, bestial creature covered in smooth, black scales. Long, white fur grew atop his head and along his back. I could easily see his magnificent musculature through his shiny scales. His face was remarkably similar to Earth canines; erect, pointed ears, a long muzzle filled with sharp teeth, a shiny black nose. His bright blue eyes were actually luminescent, which was a little unsettling in the dark, but they were quite pretty.

Standing on all fours, he was a little over three meters tall. I couldn't imagine how tall he would be were he to stand on his hind legs only.

My crew mates called him "space wolf," which seemed fitting enough. I could see the intelligence in his eyes, and I often wondered just how much he knew. He liked to observe us as we observed him. Out of all of the subjects, 774291 was among the most cooperative. He responded well to me, in particular. I often caught him staring at me from his cage, about as often as I caught myself staring at him.

The only time 774291 was in trouble was when he was horny. He would pace, staring out of his cage aggressively. His penis was huge and intimidating; no one wanted to get near him while it was exposed. I will admit to being afraid of it as well. As much as I wanted to sooth his savage lust and give him some much-needed release, his endowment was legitimately terrifying. Well over sixty centimeters long (though no one had actually measured that), thicker than my arm, wickedly curved, covered with ridges along the shaft, and all leading up to a plump, spiked tip. That part of his anatomy was very much unlike an Earth canine, it looked more like a weapon than a reproductive organ.

The Berithians had been making sex toys based on klegnar anatomy for centuries. I have even been tempted to buy one before, but something that big wouldn't fit in my footlocker. The real thing was quite a bit scarier than the toys, throbbing and dripping. Those monstrous hips attached to it didn't even look capable of gentleness. The way he stared, that hunger and lust in his eyes, added to the level of intimidation.

I was returning from a break when I heard a ruckus in my section of the holding area. Such was to be expected; keeping so many different species near one another rarely resulted in quiet. This time, however, I recognized two of the voices. 774291's howling was unmistakable, as was the shouting of security officer Meg. I rushed forward, and as soon as I rounded a corner I came upon a sight both terrifying and arousing.

Meg had come too close to the bars. She delighted in mocking the subjects, particularly the smarter ones. 774291 had a good grip on her arms; his claws had pierced her jumpsuit but not her skin. Though she didn't look injured, she was quite furious. The subject's enormous reproductive organ slid between her legs, grinding against the crotch of her uniform. 774291 was snarling with lust, desperately trying to get off by friction.

"Let go of me, motherfucker! I am going to kill you when I get free!"

I sprinted over to 774291's cage as quickly as I could. "Put her down! DOWN!"

774291 looked me in the eye, with a mixture of anger and need. I gave him a stern glare, and he obeyed my request. The monstrous alien released Meg's arms and returned to a sitting position just inside the bars, his member throbbing obscenely.

The red-headed security officer took a few steps back, clutching her arms to her chest. Then, she drew a large-caliber pistol from a hip holster and took aim at 774291. I grabbed her by the wrist and tried to divert her aim elsewhere, but she was a trained soldier and I was but a scientist.

"Don't hurt him! I won't let you!"

"Piss off, Clover. This thing tried to have his way with me! He needs to die and you know it!"

"He's just frustrated!"

"Everyone is frustrated; that's no excuse! Look at that cock; your pet monster would have killed me with that thing!"

"He's not a monster! He's a beautiful, intelligent creature, and you have no right to end his life!"

"I'm a security officer; my job is to respond to threats against the crew. That *thing* is a threat to the crew." She adjusted her aim downward. "I'm either killing him or castrating him; take your pick."

"Stop it! We're here to study these creatures, not kill them! This is your own fault for picking on the subjects like you do! If you just left them alone, things like this wouldn't happen! If you harm him or any other subject without a valid reason, don't think for a minute I won't report you to the Alliance brass for it!"

Meg glowered at me, then jerked her hands away from mine and holstered her hand-cannon. "Fine, I won't kill your precious space wolf. If you're so worried about his sexual frustration, you should just let yourself into his cage and give him some pussy. After all, we all know that's why you're here in the first place."

Meg walked off, finishing out her rounds. Before she was out of earshot, I could hear her lobbing insults at some of the other creatures. I was furious at her, not only for pointing a gun at 774291, but for what she'd said to me. Just because I'd been arrested in my past didn't mean I was eager to sleep with everything on four legs.

I glanced over at the subject's erection and blushed. It's not like I hadn't thought about it. He was a fascinating specimen, very handsome as well. There were times when I wondered if I had a bit of a crush on him. None of the other scientists assigned to this sector has measured his organ yet, nor had anyone taken a sperm sample. I smiled and decided I should probably try to do both. For science, of course.

Nervously, I stepped closer to the bars. I looked 774291 in the eyes and spoke. "If I come in, will you play nice?"

He stuck his muzzle through the bars as far as he could and licked my nose. I accepted that as a suitable answer and made my way to the instrument table. I snapped on a pair of rubber gloves, though only so I could feign professionalism if anyone saw me. Then, I grabbed a plastic cup, a cloth tape measure, and a tube of lubricant.

Hesitantly, I opened the cage door. The subject sat obediently, making no attempt to escape or attack me. I did get the feeling that he was undressing me with his eyes, though. His colossal erection did little to shake the feeling.

I pet him like I'd pet any Earth animal, feeling both his scales and his fur. He was already quite calm in my presence; my attempt to calm him further were meaningless. I unrolled the cloth measure and knelt beside him. His gargantuan penis twitched when I touched it, far more frightening up close than from afar. I laid the cloth measure along his curved length. Just under 69 centimeters long! Next, I measured the circumference of his head, the thinnest part of his shaft, and the thickest part of his shaft: 31, 28, and 34 centimeters, respectively. His meat had to be at least ten centimeters in diameter. I memorized his measurements in my head, then put down the cloth measure.

I picked up the plastic cup, and my hands began to shake. I had fantasized about jacking off this alien for a long time, but now that I was going to actually do it I was scared. After a few deep breaths, I positioned the cup in front of his tool with one hand, then grasped him with the other.

774291 growled, but made no move to stop me. I slid my hand along his length slowly, getting a feel for his texture. Aside from the ridges, he was quite smooth. I applied a little lube and began stroking his mighty meat. The subject clawed at the floor of his cage, panting hotly. Precum dribbled out of his tip into the cup, clear and musky with just a slight tinge of purple.

Once it became clear that he wasn't going to attack me, I grew more diligent in pleasuring him. I watched his cock throb with entirely unprofessional fascination. I saw the spines on his cockhead move, fanning slightly and then coming close again with each throb of his amazing pole.

My fingers curled more tightly, and I began stroking him harder. I tried to caress his entire member with each stroke. The spines on his tip snagged my glove a couple of times, so I focused more on the shaft. As his arousal grew, he began thrusting his hips. It was an incredible turn on to watch those wonderful muscles ripple under his scaled skin and to know he was fucking my hand.

I was so focused on pleasuring him that I'd forgotten all about the inevitable goal. His climactic howl startled me; I nearly dropped the cup. The spines on his cock head flared out, with his spikes all standing straight up I could see just how frighteningly long they were. He dug his claws into the floor and came for me. His mighty prick recoiled with each shot, firing thick ropes of violet alien spunk. He easily filled the cup, the remainder of his hot load washed over my gloved hand.

Feeling his rod pulse in my hand, watching him ejaculate, feeling the warmth on my hand, and knowing I did it to him nearly brought me to a climax of my own without even needing to touch myself. With great reluctance, I released him and stood up.

I put a lid on the plastic cup and gathered my cloth measure and lube, then exited 774291's cage. I wiped the specimen cup clean, then removed my gloves and threw them away. I labeled it and placed it in a vacuum tube, sending it on its way to the science lab. Then, I accessed 774291's file on the computer and updated his records with the measurements I'd taken. The numbers were almost unbelievable, I would have thought them an error myself if I hadn't held him in my hand.

After I finished updating the record, I made my rounds. Trying my best to ignore my own intense arousal, I checked each specimen in my sector for any changes or behavioral anomalies. 774291 was still quite hard, as were many of the others, but I did my best to ignore their stiff cocks. I jacked him off for my job, not for my sick fantasies. That's what I told myself, and that's what I'd tell anyone else.

I came back to him when I was finished with my rounds, though. I stared at him, and he stared at me. I couldn't take my eyes away from his erection. He spooked me with a low yowl, a sad and almost pained noise. He was begging me to touch him again; this poor creature needed me.

I checked the schedule and saw that no one else should be through the area for at least an hour. Satisfied that I wouldn't be caught, I removed my glasses and stuck them in the pocket of my lab coat. Against my better judgment, I stripped down just outside 774291's bars. He watched intently as I bared myself to him, quite interested in my human anatomy. I left my clothes just outside his cage, where I could reach them if I needed to, and went inside.

The subject nuzzled between my luscious breasts and licked me from sternum to nose. Then he licked each of my nipples with his gigantic tongue, fanning the flames of my lust. He next nuzzled between my legs and licked my pussy hard. I shivered, almost collapsed. His tongue had a rough surface, covered in tiny bony spines like a cat's. The feel of it on my sensitive vulva was indescribable.

I lay down on the floor of the cage, offering myself to my alien lover. He gently placed a paw on my belly and began to lick my pussy. I bucked my hips and moaned for him. My body jerked every time that rough, strong tongue stroked across my needy nethers. His licks came even faster once he decided he liked my flavor. I could tell he was trying to get his tongue inside me, but it just wasn't firm enough to penetrate my tightness. The hard, directed licks were definitely having an effect, though.

I stroked his fur and scales while he devoured my slavering pink place. I wanted so badly to hold out and make it last, but I knew that to be impossible. The instant his tongue grazed my erect clit, I lost it. With a scream, I came for him. He enthusiastically lapped up my juices, his reward for a job well done.

After I came, he spent a while "cleaning"

me. I twitched and gasped with every slurp, supersensitive to his scratchy tongue. Once all of my fluids had been licked up, he rose up and stood over the top of me. That gargantuan cock hung down between his legs, pulsing and dripping precum. The thought of putting that inside any part of my body made me want to scream.

Despite my fear, I stood and bent completely over, putting my hands on the floor and holding my ass high in the air. He took a step towards me, and then his cock lurched forward to rub against my pussy; the head slipped back and forth across my slit, grinding between my thighs one moment and between my buns the next. Finally, he found the mark and nudged my folds apart with just the very tip.

"Please, be gentle."

774291 was indeed gentle with me. He prodded my pussy with his enormous cock until I loosened up a little. He wedged himself into me little by little, taking me very slowly and patiently. I cried out in a mixture of pleasure and pain with every movement, feeling my pussy spread open wider than ever before.

My body quivered as more and more of that mind-boggling sex organ disappeared between my folds. I screamed a little with every push, fearing I would split in half at any moment. Despite my apparent capacity for girth, my body would accept no more than ten inches of length. His mighty dick prodded my cervix once the limit was met, and I screamed in pain. He craned his neck to lick me and drew back a little. Once he was satisfied that I was okay, he pulled out a bit more.

His spines fanned out with the backward motion and scratched the inside of my pussy all along the way. To my surprise, the feeling was actually quite pleasurable. His dick spikes weren't as sharp as they looked and had a sensation like a more extreme version of his tongue. He pulled back until only the head was inside. The very instant he began pushing back into me, I came again.

My pussy rippled along my alien lover's incredible girth and my juices splashed all over his magnificent organ. He took me in slow, tender strokes. I came with almost every thrust, stacking up more orgasms than I ever thought possible.

As I relaxed more for him and we both became increasingly wet, he began to speed up. Just a little at a time, the increase in pace was very gradual and easy. I gritted my teeth and trembled, barely able to remain standing. The faster he moved, the more often I came. The spines, ridges, and sheer size of his penis ensured I would never be satisfied by anything from my home planet again. I was definitely buying one of those Berithian klegnar dildos; there was simply no way not to.

Soon enough he was breeding me at a respectably swift pace, pounding that huge boner in and out of my flooded pussy. Every thrust into me made our mixed fluids splash over my bare ass, every pull-out with those lovely spikes made me cum again and add to the moisture. All thought of professionalism or consequences left my mind. He was fucking me so good, I couldn't even think straight!

The thrusts came faster and faster, and the sex became even more satisfying. My body was soon so flooded with endorphins that I couldn't feel anything at all. I was so lost in pleasure that I didn't even recognize it. I experienced orgasm after orgasm after orgasm. I began to feel dehydrated, but I didn't care. I was this alien's bitch now, and I intended to stay for the full ride.

When he finally did cum, it felt too soon. I wanted so much more of him. He pressed as deep as he possibly could, mashing his head firmly against my cervix. His spines flared out in all directions and he roared in climactic bliss. My scream joined his discordant wail as I came one more time with him. He pumped an ocean of cum into me, filling my womb beyond capacity and spilling the excess out of my stretched pussy. I could feel hot cum running down my thighs and back, all over me. It was so hot on my bare skin, it almost felt like it was burning me.

774291 held himself in until he was dry, then pulled out. I came again when those spines popped out of me, barely able to gasp when I did. I stood on shaky, rubbery legs and looked at my lover. He was lying down with a great big smile, quite sated. I stumbled out of his cage and locked the door behind me. Something felt wrong. I told myself I was just oversexed, but my belly was cramping and I felt genuinely ill. I heard a noise and looked back at my lover; he seemed concerned now. His pretty blue eyes were the last thing I saw before I blacked out.

I awoke several hours later in a daze. My entire lower body hurt in ways I didn't even think were possible. My pussy wasn't just sore; it was on fire. I felt like I'd been submerged in molten lead. I realized that I'd been crying out in pain the entire time I'd been awake, perhaps even a bit before.

Medical officer Kelly came over and renewed my morphine drip, making the agony fade after a few seconds. She had a peculiar combination of annoyance, disgust, and intrigue on her face. I tried to sit up, but winced and fell back onto the medical bed.

"What happened? Where am I?"

"You're in the infirmary, being treated for poisoning and internal blisters."

"Wait, what?"

"Thanks to you, we now know that subject number 774291's semen is extremely toxic to humans." Her tone was gut-wrenchingly sarcastic. "Contact with exposed skin causes severe burns and blistering; absorption into the body causes organ damage on par with some of Earth's strongest toxins. That is not proper scientific method, by the way. What respectable science officer has sex with an alien creature we know practically nothing about and allows him to inject unknown substances into her?"

"Don't you judge me! Some humans mate with Berithians, is that wrong?"

"Yes, I think that it is. But Berithian semen doesn't poison humans. You almost killed yourself back there; I hope it was worth it."

"For your information, it was worth it. Making love to him felt better than...wait, where is he? Is he okay?"

"Yes, he's fine. Better than usual, even. After what you did, he's sleeping better and behaving even more calmly than before. As much as your method perplexes me, I can't really argue with the results. I just can't recommend doing that again; you may not get so lucky next time. If not for a timely blood transfusion, you'd be dead right now. In the future, don't put alien semen into any of your orifices until it's been examined and tested!"

"How bad are my internal burns? Will I ever be able to have sex again?"

"Yes, you'll be fine. There was no permanent damage, though you'll be in a great deal of pain until you've recovered. The burns and blisters should heal within a couple of weeks. I'd rather not see you in here for the same thing again, though. Please try to be more careful in your disgusting hobbies."

I frowned, but said nothing. Kelly took good care of me during my time in the infirmary, though she ridiculed me harshly all throughout. Word spread, and I became the laughing stock of most of the ship. On the plus side, the propositions for lesbian sex mostly stopped.

The effects of 774291's semen on my body had been dutifully recorded and in great detail. The science lab emailed me a document listing the test results of the semen samples from various alien species. It was their job to run these tests on all collected bodily fluids, but the results weren't an important part of anyone else's job. The document was boldly labeled "FOR THE SAFETY AND WELL-BEING OF ALL OF NEO-ARK'S CREW," but it didn't take long to figure out they'd sent the document only to me.

The calming effect I had on the subjects was definitely desirable, though. Despite the mockery of my crew mates, I was providing a valuable service. Armed with a list of potential dangers and the knowledge that I couldn't be outed twice, I began regularly servicing all of the subjects in my sector. I had to make some wear condoms, though they hardly seemed to mind that for a chance to get off. Some of their penises were just too oddly shaped or dangerous to put inside me, so I pleasured them with my hands or breasts as well as I could. I even experimented with pleasuring the female subjects, I liked getting them off, but it was never as much fun as mating with the males.

No matter how much alien sex I had though, none could ever satisfy my lust or touch my heart the way 774291 had. I often slept in his cage, cuddled up with him. Sometimes I allowed him to take me unprotected, though I made sure he pulled out well before cumming. I endured the burns when he came on me; I didn't care that it hurt. As long as he didn't get any inside me, it was fine.

My sector became one of the most peaceful and mellow on the entire ship. My diligent efforts had erased all traces of sexual frustration among my assigned subjects. When word reached the Alliance brass, not only of my actions but also my results, I was awarded two medals. One was silver planet for "extraordinary bravery in contact with extraterrestrial species," normally reserved for soldiers fighting in wars against aliens. The other was a retroactive purple heart with regards to my injuries from the first night with 774291. Some smart-ass edited my personnel file to list subject number 774291 as my husband in the Alliance database. A stupid joke, sure. But if the shoe fits, wear it.

8 A HIDDEN GIFT

I sat in bed, staring at the wall, waiting.

My lover, Sarah, had locked herself in the bathroom. Every time I asked her for sex, she would run off and hide. We had been together for about six months and never got farther than kissing. She would typically come out of hiding after about an hour and act like nothing happened.

This time was different, though. Sarah let herself out of the bathroom after only about twenty minutes. The shapely brunette nervously returned to the bedroom. She sat on the corner of the bed, facing away from me. I could tell that she was very tense, but I couldn't begin to guess why.

"Jean, sweetie, we need to talk."

I frowned. "About what? What's going on?"

"I haven't been honest with you. I feel terrible for not telling you everything, but it's hard to say."

"You know you can tell me anything, Sarah."

She hesitated for a long moment before speaking. "Jean, I'm not entirely human."

"Of course you are!"

"No, I'm not. I'm...well, have you ever seen those perverted Japanese cartoons? The kind with tentacles?"

"Don't change the subject!"

"I'm not. Tentacle monsters are real."

"Are you trying to tell me you're a goddamn cartoon octopus?"

"Kind of. My mother was attacked by tentacles, before I was born. They impregnated her, and she gave birth to a hybrid child. That tentacle-human hybrid is me."

"Bullshit! You do not have tentacles!"

"Will you take me seriously for just a minute? You have no idea how hard it is to share something like this!"

"Well, how am I supposed to react?"

"I don't know, but you could at least try to be supportive!"

I sighed heavily. "You're right, I'm sorry."

"Thank you."

"So tell me. How, exactly, are you different from an ordinary person?"

"Most of the time, I'm not. It's only when I'm aroused that things start getting weird. My fluids turn into tentacles."

"That sounds messy."

"Well, it is. Very messy, actually. You're taking this better than I thought you would."

"I'm sorry, babe, I still don't really believe

you."

"What do you want me to do?"

"Show them to me."

"Then what happens? What if you're wrong and I actually have them?"

"I'll let you put them inside me."

"Really?"

"Sure! I've wanted to do it with you since the moment we met. If a little tentacle molestation is all that's keeping us apart, I can handle it. It might even be kind of fun."

Sarah stood up and removed her panties, then crawled up onto the bed. She sat opposite from me, with her back against the footboard. Her legs were open wide; I saw her exposed muff for the first time. She had a small patch of pubes shaved into a lightning bolt, which pointed directly to her pink place.

I watched Sarah stroke her puffy, pink lips with two fingers. As deeply as she was blushing, I could tell she hadn't done this in front of anyone before. After a few seconds, I started to see some moisture. My lover penetrated herself with two fingers and pumped vigorously. I slipped a hand into my own panties and joined her. Even if the tentacle story was an obvious lie, letting me watch is the furthest she had ever gone.

Sarah's mound quickly grew wetter in response to the stimulation. Soon, she was literally dripping. She pulled her fingers free and tasted herself. Before my very eyes, the moisture on her petals congealed. Her fluid formed a slim tendril, about three inches long and no wider than my pinkie.

I watched with rapt fascination as the clear tentacle undulated in the air. Its entire surface glistened in the dim light. The pillar of liquid danced for me, and my eyes followed its every motion.

"That's amazing! Does it move on its own or can you control it?"

"I have complete control of it; it's a part of my body."

"Is there any sensation in it?"

"I can feel everything it feels."

"Can I touch it?"

Sarah blushed deeply, but nodded. I crawled across the bed and cautiously reached for the tentacle. Its surface was slick and wet; touching it got pussy juice on my fingers. The tentacle wrapped around one of my fingers and gently squeezed, then uncurled. It slowly grew longer and thicker while I played with it.

"It's getting bigger."

"It's made of pussy juice. The wetter I get, the bigger I can make it. If I get wet enough, I can make more than one at a time."

"Does touching it turn you on?" "Yes, my tentacles are as sensitive as my clit."

I grinned evilly and squeezed the tentacle tight. Sarah gasped and bucked her hips. I loosened my grip and stroked the tentacle swiftly. It grew in my hand, then split into two tentacles. Each was about an inch across.

I continued to jack off one tentacle, but wrapped my lips around the other. It had a sweet, musky flavor. The tip poked around the inside of my mouth, exploring me. I sucked and licked, swallowing the juices that came off of the surface. My free hand drifted down to tease my own muff.

I gagged a little when Sarah's tentacle prodded the back of my throat. Fortunately, she pulled it back. The tentacle in my hand grew a little thicker, elongating as it did so. It was soon too long for me to see the tip without turning my head. A few minutes later, I felt something wet nudge itself between my fingers and slither up into my pussy.

I moaned hotly around the mouthful of solidified muff juice. The wet tentacle easily penetrated my drooling pussy. It was made of lubricant and mixed with some of my own cream to create a very slick sensation. It probed deeper and deeper, until I had to grunt to let Sarah know she was going too far. She stopped pushing inward and instead began to thrust. I could feel it growing thicker, spreading me wider and wider around its incredibly slick surface.

The stimulation proved to be too much for Sarah, who soon came. Her hips bucked, and an adorable squeak escaped her lips. Both of her tentacles fired hot streams of girl-cum into me. I moaned and greedily swallowed all she could give. The sensation of her cumming in my pussy gave me tingles.

I continued to lick and suck her tentacle, making her squirm and tremble. After a few seconds, her other tentacle resumed thrusting in and out of my pussy. She formed a third tentacle, which swelled to about an inch thick and then began to grow in length. I wasn't made to wonder where it was going for long. I soon felt the tip poke my anus.

My puckered sphincter clenched reflexively, but the wet warmth did feel nice. Sarah's tentacle teased my butt until I relaxed a little and then wedged itself inside. I had never done anal play before; the sensation was very strange.

Sarah tested my ass for comfortable depth. I grunted again to let her know she'd gone far enough. She alternated thrusts; pushing into my pussy as she pulled out of my ass and vice versa. The feel of something thrusting into my bottom, especially something so warm and wet, was one of the most peculiar sensations I have ever experienced.

The ass-probing tentacle grew thicker until it matched the girth of its twin in my pussy. I moaned hotly around the shorter tentacle in my mouth. Another tentacle sprouted; this one remained very thin. It grew long very quickly and moved to wrap itself around my clit. It tugged my sensitive nub, and I let out a muffled scream.

My body shook uncontrollably, and my fluids flowed freely onto Sarah's slippery coils. Sarah came again just as I was finishing my climax, squirting more of her sweet juices into me. The excess fluids ran down my thighs. I was becoming very wet and sticky.

Two more slim tentacles appeared and gave my nipples the same treatment my clit was receiving. They alternated their tugs, pulling on one nipple and then the other. My clit got a firm tug in between the nipple tugs. Another large tentacle grew and pressed itself between my breasts. The slick, slimy warmth on my bare flesh sent tingles all through my body.

The more she did to me, the more it stimulated her, and the faster her tentacles could grow. She formed four thick ones at the same time and coiled one around each of my arms and legs. The tentacle in my mouth pulled itself out, much to my disappointment.

Sarah hoisted me into the air, easily lifting me above the bed. Her slippery tentacles continued their wonderful ministrations, even as I was moved further away. I was held spread-eagle about five feet above the bed. The tentacle that had been in my mouth grew thicker and then began to anally penetrate Sarah.

"This is amazing! How can your pussy juice be this strong?"

"I don't know. There's no muscle in the

tentacles themselves, and I never feel muscle strain anywhere else from using them. All it takes is concentration. Physically, it's effortless. I think I could lift a car with them if I tried."

The tentacle that was tit-fucking me pressed a little further forward and poked my chin. I tilted my head down and opened my mouth, gladly accepting one of Sarah's sweet-tasting juice tentacles into my mouth again. I suckled while it enthusiastically thrusted between my breasts and into my mouth.

The position Sarah held me in gave me a great view of what she was doing to herself. She lay flat on her back, playing with her tits and tentacle fucking herself in the ass. Her eyes drifted from my crotch to my breasts, then back to my crotch. She formed another plump tentacle and slid it between her own boobs, then into her mouth.

Sarah made the tentacle in her rump grow until it was of absurd girth. It had to be at least five inches across when it finally stopped. Looking through the clear tentacle, I could see inside her ass from five feet away. I could also see her belly bulge with every slow thrust she made into herself. I could tell from her quiet screams and the goofy look on her face that she was into stretching. I made a mental note to get both of my arms inside her, at some point.

It wasn't long until Sarah came again. Two new tentacles formed, each about two inches thick. They made their way up to me and one wedged into each hole. I moaned deeply around the tentacle in my mouth. They were stretching me wide, but the slipperiness helped me enjoy it.

The tentacles moved rapidly. One slid into my pussy just as the other pulled out, the same happened in my ass. Sarah and I shared a wonderful simultaneous orgasm. Our muffled screams blended together beautifully.

All of the tentacles penetrating me, even the one in my mouth, grew thicker. The thrusting came faster, making me writhe and scream in the air. Sarah released her breasts and grabbed at the sheets instead. I could see her eyes roll back and her body tremble. She was overloading herself. No new tentacles formed. Her excess juice dribbled down onto the bed.

I couldn't handle much more and soon came again. Sarah finished soon after I did. This time, though, all of her tentacles suddenly turned back into juice. I fell to the bed with a gurgled scream, nearly choking around a sudden mouthful of liquid. The sheets were soaking wet. My entire body was covered in slick juices, as was hers.

After a few deep breaths, Sarah propped herself up on her elbows. "Are you okay?"

"Yeah, I'm fine. Are you okay?"

"Yes, just tired. I'm sorry I dropped you. It takes a lot of focus to form the tentacles and keep them solid. I usually only use them to molest myself. I'm not accustomed to using them on another person. So much pleasure, all at once! I just lost my concentration."

"I'm surprised you managed to keep them

together as long as you did and to have that kind of coordination! I can't focus on anything when I'm having an orgasm."

"I learned a lot about controlling them when I was a teenager."

I laughed and then crawled over to the other end of the bed. Sarah wrapped her arms and legs around me. I held her close, and we shared a deep kiss. The taste of her tentacles was still heavy on her own breath; I assumed the same of my own. We were both in dire need of a shower, but I was just too tired.

"Thank you for not running away. It means a lot to me that you're still here."

"Thanks for trusting me with your secret. That was a lot of fun! I wouldn't mind doing that again, some time."

"I love you, Jean."

"I love you, too, Sarah."

We held each other tightly and went to sleep. In the morning, we woke up very sticky. After peeling apart, we made our way to the shower. Her tentacles came out to play again while we were washing, though this session was far milder. Just one orgasm each before we prepared to part ways for the day for work.

Sarah and I continued to have semi-regular tentacle sex sessions from then on. She got better at controlling multiple tentacles, and her use of them became more creative. On more than one occasion, we involved a third woman in our lovemaking. Sarah always made sure that everyone got off, plenty of times.

9 SIN AND PUNISHMENT

Heavy chains bound my wrists and ankles. Armed guards led me by my elbows through a dim corridor. I had been caught stealing, yet again. I knew the punishment well, having experienced it more times than I could count. A cool breeze blew through the stone corridor, sending a chill through my nude body and erecting my exposed nipples.

Yokan was considered a strange land by many outsiders. Its people lived in shame and fear of their own libidos. Sexuality was so thoroughly stigmatized that the most effective punishments involved sexual humiliation. The penalty for theft was mild, compared to some of the harsher crimes. Mild enough that I never really mind being caught.

The guardsmen brought me into a large central chamber. Sunlight filtered through stained glass windows depicting the gods. The light formed a patchwork of colorful shapes on the white marble floor. Priestess Morinth waited near the center of the room. I recognized her; she had punished me three times in a row. She was tall and graceful, with lovely blonde hair and sparkly green eyes. She wore the typical black vestments, and wielded a long pole that was topped with a painted wooden phallus.

I was brought before the priestess and thrown to the floor. One of the guards grabbed me be the hair and made me sit up to look at Morinth. The lovely priestess frowned down at me. She looked disappointed, as though she honestly expected me to change my ways. Most people would certainly have done so by now, the men especially. I was one of those peculiar individuals with a resistance to punishment.

"Daena, you have been found guilty of theft," said Morinth. "The gods look down upon you in contempt for your actions. What have you to say for yourself?"

"I have wronged my fellow citizens and I am deserving of harsh punishment. I am ready for my sentence."

"Very well. Guards, leave the room. Thief, on your hands and knees."

It was slightly awkward moving with the chains, but I was very familiar with the position. I held my butt up in the air, awaiting my punishment. As soon as the guards left, Morinth slapped my ass with the dildo-spear. I gasped and wiggled, making no attempt to hide my enjoyment.

The priestess anointed the wooden cock with sacred oils. Once the faux phallus was shiny and fragrant, the priestess poked it between my cheeks. She teased my pucker momentarily, and then shoved the polished dildo inside. I let out a long moan, and accepted every inch of the wooden cock. My rump was quite accustomed to such abuse. I felt nothing but pleasure from the deep penetration.

Morinth jabbed in and out harshly, thrusting the toy into my rump as though it were a real spear. I moaned with every powerful thrust. Her arms were a lot stronger than they looked. That's why Morinth was my favorite priestess. Not that I ever got to choose who punished me, but if given the choice I would pick her. The others either lacked her strength or refused to make use of it, I was never sure which.

My arms trembled beneath me. It was hard to hold myself up while getting buggered so well. Soon, my arms gave out and my upper body hit the floor. The cold marble pressing against my nipples turned me on even more. Cloudy nectar dripped from my pussy. I was intensely aroused already, but it would take me a while to climax from anal stimulation alone.

The thrusts grew harder, and my moans got louder. I couldn't tell if she was getting angry, or if she just wanted to get me off faster. Involuntary orgasms were supposed to be an incredibly shameful experience, hence their use as punishment. It was never involuntary when it happened to me, though. Anal play was also taboo and supposedly shameful, but I saw it as a blessing from the gods themselves.

My panting grew continually heavier, my moans grew louder. The punishment chamber's acoustics were fantastic. I was getting hornier by the second, hearing the reverb of my own sex noises. Morinth's arms never stopped moving. The brutal priestess tore my ass up in the best of ways.

Suddenly, the tip of the dildo popped free of my stretched anus. Before I could ask what was happening, Morinth shoved it back inside.I gasped and squeezed tight, but she pulled it out again. Each time, she left me empty just long enough for my ass to close up a little. Then, she roughly rammed it back inside.

After a few minutes of that treatment, she shoved the toy deep and left it there. Gripping the spear in both hands, she began to thrust it faster and harder than I'd ever taken it before. My voice rose into a loud, continuous scream. If she was trying to hurt me, it wasn't working. The sacred oils were very slick, and made a fantastic lubricant. I found it hard to believe that the gods condemned my actions when one of their servants was bringing me such pleasure.

In just minutes, I was brought to a very intense orgasm. My entire body trembled, and a mighty wail of ecstasy echoed down the corridors. My pussy squirted a high pressure stream of girl cum onto the floor and Morinth's robes. She kept pounding the toy in and out of me after I came, making me writhe on the floor.

All too soon, Morinth stopped and pulled the wooden cock out of my ass. I nearly protested, but held my silence. Things could get incredibly awkward if I told her I wanted this. Better to just steal something and get in trouble again. She put her spear on a holding rack, then knelt down and rolled me onto my back. The priestess looked me in the eye with a stern expression.

"Daena, you have paid your debt to the gods. I hope I do not have to see you here again."

"Oh priestess, I have learned my lesson. You shame me with the pleasures you bring, I am so embarrassed! Never again will I steal."

"Do not lie to me, girl."

"Lie? Perish the thought! Is this not normally the part where you unchain me?"

"You have no shame, it is easy to see. You derive pleasure from what I do to you, and you make no attempt to hide it."

"That is ridiculous. I am filled with shame, just like everyone else."

"Do you know what place our society has for shameless women?"

"Of course. None."

"You are wrong. The order of priestesses knows no shame."

"That cannot be true! You punish with shame."

"Exactly. The job of a priestess is to touch, molest, and embarrass. We cannot feel shame for our actions, or else our performance would suffer. To punish sinners, we must be devoid of sexual shame in ourselves. You would do well in the order, I think."

"I will consider what you have said. I am usually on the opposite side of the law, though."

"Did I mention that priestess training involves lots of sexual practice with the other priestesses? You would be learning methods of punishment on them, and they would learn on you."

"Where do I sign up?"

Morinth laughed.

"I will take you to the head priestess; she will want to interview you before offering you training. But first, I would like to sample you for myself."

Morinth stood and shed her robes. The flowing vestments came off easily and fell to the floor. I gawked up at her beautiful, nude body. Her loose clothing hid a vision of curvaceous glory. I caught myself salivating as my eyes explored her sculpted thighs and succulent hips.

I was allowed to stare for only a moment before the priestess broke her stillness. In the blink of an eye, she was upon me. Her glistening pink prize hovered just above my face. I could tell the punishment ritual had excited her greatly.

Just before my tongue could sample the dew from her petals, Morinth pressed down. Her crotch mashed against my face, smearing her slippery nectar over my lips. I didn't hesitate to wedge my tongue between her folds. My licks came hard and fast, coaxing moans of approval from the priestess. Her vocalizations encouraged me to work even harder at pleasing her.

After a few seconds of tongue lashing her slit, I felt Morinth lean forward. Her new position took some of the pressure off of my face and let me move around a bit more. I used the newfound freedom of motion to launch a direct assault on her stiff clitoris.

The priestess rewarded my efforts by burying her face between my legs and sliding her hot tongue across my drooling snatch. I could tell she was very experienced. Her licks and nibbles were all just right, and sent tremors of lust through my body. It wasn't surprising; her job was to know how to set someone off.

I upped the ante, trying my hardest to emulate the wonderful pleasures she was giving me. Just when I thought I was matching her lick for lick, Morinth pressed two fingers into my ass. My anus was still slick with sacred oils, and her digits penetrated me easily. With my hands bound, I had no way of returning the gesture.

I used my tongue and lips as well as I knew how. Morinth added a third finger, furthering the edge she had over me. Soon, she wedged her pinkie in as well. I squirmed and whimpered. Slick muff sauce drooled freely from my mound. The crowded feeling in my backside made it a little hard to focus on the task before me.

When Morinth pushed her whole hand into my ass, I lost it. Screaming and bucking my hips, I came all over the priestess's face. Morinth chuckled above me and lifted herself free before I could get another lick of her sweetness. She unshackled me, and then stood up.

"Not bad. You have potential, you will be better with some practice."

"Don't you want me to finish you off?"

"Another time, perhaps. For now, let's get you cleaned up for the interview."

The meeting with the head priestess went well. I was accepted into the order and excelled in my training. I was able to bring the other priestesses to orgasm easily, much to their delight. I learned all of the different methods of sexual punishment, how to use my mouth, my fingers, my fists, various toys, paddles, bondage gear and even the complicated sex machines used for punishing serious crimes. The largest of them required three priestesses rotating a wheel simultaneously to function.

After becoming a full priestess, I swiftly became known as one of the most feared disciplinarians in all of Yokan. Not only was I able to bring vast amounts of unwanted pleasure to sinners, but I had mastered the art of humiliating dirty talk as well. The typical delicate sensibilities couldn't handle it; I broke criminals down into law-abiding citizens with ease.

As an unfortunate side-effect, the crime rate began to drop. My reputation grew to the point that my job became far less active. I got to punish someone every now and then, but not as often as I liked. I had to turn to the other priestesses for fun in between sinners.

A few years later, I was made to punish a girl who moaned a bit too much and blushed a bit too little. My dirty talk had the curious effect of just making her hornier. After that first punishment, I saw her again and again. She not only continued her crime spree, she got sloppy about it. She got caught intentionally, just to be punished by me.

Once I was certain of her intentions, I told her what Morinth had told me years before. I talked to the head priestess, and secured the girl's acceptance into the order. I volunteered to train her personally, and I was not denied that request.

10 SEEING SPOTS

The soles of my shoes impacted the rubber-topped running track, sending little shock waves through my aching legs. I'd been running for so long, I'd lost track of time. My lungs burned, my legs hurt, and my feet threatened to secede from my body. I ran to the point of feeling ill, trying to keep up with my girlfriend.

Amber made it look so easy. She'd maintained the same even, steady pace for what seemed like hours. She didn't look exhausted. She had barely even broken a sweat. I seethed with envy at her incredible endurance.

When I could take no more, I marched myself over to the bleachers and plopped down. All of the schools were abandoned for the summer, so the two of us had commandeered the track course behind a middle school for a fun-run. It was her idea, of course. I liked to stay in shape, but I couldn't fathom the idea of exercise being "fun." I stole a bottle of water from her gym bag and watched her run.

After three more effortless laps around the track, Amber slowed to a walk and approached me. Her black Lycra shorts clung to her like a second skin, leaving little to the imagination. Her white cotton tank top had become sweaty in just the right places, achieving selective transparency and showing off her lack of a sports bra. Not that she needed one. As a shapeshifter, she never had to worry about sagging.

"All done, Evan?"

"Babe, if I run any more, I'm going to die."

She laughed. "I doubt that, Captain Hyperbole." She sat down next to me and took a water bottle for herself from the gym bag. "You did pretty well. I didn't expect you to last that long."

"I tried, but I just can't keep up with you."

"Oh, of course you can't. I can run forever."

"What?"

"One of my abilities is unlimited stamina. Since my body can re-shape itself, I never have to worry about strain and fatigue. My muscles are in a constant state of readiness."

"That's cheating."

"Maybe, but I never said it was a contest."

"True."

I leaned back, resting my head on the bleacher behind me. A cool breeze blew, soothing my overtaxed body. My grey T-shirt was soaked through with sweat, and my basketball shorts felt swampy inside.

After a few moments of silence, Amber spoke. "Hey, remember that furry picture you found on the Internet?"

"Which one?"

"That leopard girl. You thought she had a really nice ass?"

"Yeah, what about her?"

"She looked about like this, right?"

I opened my eyes, and nearly jumped out of my skin. Amber had shifted into an anthropomorphic leopardess. She had removed her shoes and socks, allowing her feet to shift into digitigrade paws, but her shorts and top remained. Her breasts had grown substantially. The tank top strained to hold them. She had shifted into animals before, but I had never seen her turn into a zoanthrope.

"You're shifting in public? Are you crazy?"

"Pfft, what public? We haven't seen anybody all day! And besides, I'm a goddamn jungle cat! Nobody is going to mess with us!"

Amber stood and turned away from me. With one swift motion, she bent over and pulled her shorts to the ground. Tail held high, she wiggled her amazing ass at me. I couldn't resist touching it. I ran my fingers through her fur, feeling the incredible softness. My dick grew rock hard in seconds.

"How does it look? Did I get the curvature right?"

"It's perfect, just the way I remember. This seems kind of random, though."

She stood and shrugged. "I'm feeling feline today. I remembered you liked that picture, so I thought I'd pick a form that's good for us both."

Amber peeled off her top and tossed it aside, exposing her luscious breasts. She straddled me, putting those furry melons in my face. I nuzzled into her cleavage and reached up to grasp her white-furred globes. My fingers teased her nipples while I inhaled the musky scent from her fluffy chest fur.

I could feel her grinding her crotch against mine. My member ached for release, straining against the fabric of my shorts. She teased me cruelly, grinding very lightly and then pulling away when I tried to grind back.

Suddenly, she leaned back and took her bosoms away from my face. Those beautiful blue eyes of hers locked onto mine and she leaned in for a kiss. Her long, rough tongue slipped into my mouth. I slid my tongue along hers and appreciated her attention to detail. In turning herself into a were-leopard, she had made her tongue into a startling facsimile of a cat's barbed tongue. Just as the idea of oral sex entered my head, she broke the kiss. It was sometimes easy to forget that her abilities included mind-reading. She put her furry hands on my shoulders and guided me to lie down on the bleachers. She then positioned herself over me, holding her glistening pussy above my face.

I grasped her hips and pressed my face into her crotch without hesitation. She'd retained a human-like pussy this time, to my surprise. Though, given that the differences between female mammals weren't exactly staggering, I decided it was more important what the pussy is attached to.

My tongue slipped between her folds, collecting her sweet nectar. She was always so very flavorful for me. Cunnilingus was one of my favorite things to do, which I think was her intention. While I tasted her, she casually stroked my erection through my shorts. Once she was through teasing me, she pulled my shorts down and set my boner free. My just-below-average pole throbbed hotly in the humid air. That rough, feline tongue of hers pressed against the base of my cock. Then, she slid it all the way to the tip in one long, slow lick. I tried to concentrate on munching leopard carpet, but the feel of her prickly tongue on my meat had me squirming. When that wonderful tongue reached my glans, I pulled away from her crotch to moan out loud.

She swirled her tongue in swift circles around the very tip of my cock. I writhed beneath her, helpless to do more than moan. Pre-cum dribbled from my straining prick, only to be swiftly licked up by the horny were-leopard on top of me.

It took some willpower, but I managed to resume licking Amber's slippery leopard cooch. I concentrated on her clit, trying to return some of the pleasure she was giving me. I knew I couldn't come close to the sensation her roughness provided, so I tried to compensate with swift flicks of my tongue.

I kneaded her fantastic ass in my hands. The anthro-leopard's furry bottom felt better than I could have ever imagined. My fingers drifted to the crevice beneath her tail. I felt around between her cheeks until I found her tight pucker. She clenched when I touched it. I tickled her anus teasingly, feeling her squirm above me.

The were-leopard cupped my balls and attacked my cock even more fervently. That long, scratchy tongue coiled along the entire length of my shaft. Her pink oral organ wriggled around my sensitive pole, scraping exquisitely with even the slightest motion.

I took my fingers away from her virgin ass, and instead teased it with the tip of my tongue. My fingers took over where my mouth had left off. I firmly pushed two digits into her slavering mound. My touch gravitated to her G-spot immediately. I stroked her clit with my thumb, earning soft moans from my sexy leopardess.

After a few teasing licks, her anus began to relax. I wormed my tongue inside and felt her flex around it. My fingers pumped in and out of her juicy muff faster. I pushed my tongue deep into her exquisite ass.

I didn't have to work her over for long to

finish her off. Amber pulled her tongue from my rod and cried out in bliss. Her hot fluids splashed onto my neck. I continued to pump my fingers until her orgasmic flexes died down. I slowly withdrew my digits from her sopping-wet snatch and teasingly stroked her labia.

Amber resumed licking my pole. Her tongue lashed across my sensitive cockhead again and again. The wonderful tingles grew more and more intense as I approached orgasm. When I got close, she stopped licking. She stroked instead, vigorously jacking me off with her furry hand.

It didn't take me long to reach the finish line. I bucked my hips and let out a grunt. My seed spurted out in thin ribbons, laying cummy streaks across her face. The last of my load dribbled down the side of my cock. She licked me clean, making me squirm from oversensitivity.

Amber turned around and kissed me on the lips, letting me taste a little of my own salty spunk. She had white stripes across her face now, which was actually a good look for her. After breaking the kiss, she turned away from me again. This time, she got on all fours in the grass.

I knelt behind her and grasped her hips. Without hesitation, I lined up with her glistening petals and slid my modest length inside her. She moaned and pressed her rump back to me. I bred her in short, fast thrusts. The feel of her wet heat grasping me was exquisite.

After a few seconds, my body reminded me just how exhausted and sore I actually was. I pulled out and returned to the bleachers. She twisted around to cast me a concerned gaze.

"Is something wrong?"

"I'm just too tired."

"Oh, poor baby. Want me to do all the work?"

"That would be great."

Amber stood and came close to me. She put a hand on my chest and gently guided me to lean back as far as possible. The anthropomorphic jungle cat placed a knee on each side of me and straddled my lap. I felt her tits squish against my chest just before she kissed me again.

She rubbed her pussy teasingly against my still-hard dick for a few seconds. Our lips parted for a mutual moan when my glans slipped between her glistening petals. She easily took my full length, sitting in my lap and grinding her crotch against mine.

That beautiful leopard began to move, swiveling her immaculate hips atop my body. I watched my cock appear and disappear between her pink petals. I could see her muscles rippling beneath that spotted, tan fur. The form she'd chosen was truly exquisite; animalistic enough to fan the flames of my lust, but human enough for conventional positions.

My hands rest on her hips momentarily before sliding around to cup her glorious buttocks. She rewarded my touch with tight clenches, making me groan and squirm. The best thing about sex with a shapeshifter is that she was always the perfect tightness, no matter what form she took.

My fingers found her saliva-slicked asshole and resumed the teasing tickle I had put on hold earlier. This time, I didn't stop at touching the rim. I gently pushed a finger into her tight bum. She shivered and let out a quiet moan, but didn't break rhythm.

I slowly worked my finger in and out of her tight butt while she bounced on my dick. I could feel her hard nipples grind against my chest through the thin fabric of my t-shirt. She moved her hands from my shoulders to the bleacher behind me. Grasping the metal firmly, she began moving her magnificent body even faster.

Amber's ass squeezed my finger tightly while her pussy massaged my hard dick. I soon added a second digit, making her gasp. I sped up my fingering, trying to match the pace she set. Her claws dug into the metal on either side of my head, further enhancing her grip.

I pulled my mouth off of her nipple so I could speak. "Are you going to cum?"

"Getting there."

"Roar for me."

"No, it'll sound silly."

"Please?"

"I'll try, but only because you're such a good lay."

I slapped her furry ass with my free hand and then wedged a third finger into her tight hole. That was enough to set her off. Amber threw her head back and screamed, doing her best impression of a big cat's roar. Her flexing pussy massaged my tool just right. I came seconds after her, spilling my hot seed into her depths. She timed her flexes, milking me dry.

After she'd taken all I could give, she rest on top of me for a little while. I pulled my fingers out of her butt and stroked her back. She kissed me and held her body close to mine. After a little while, she stood up. I could see a few pearly white droplets oozing down from her pink pussy.

"I'm going to run a little more while you rest up for the walk home."

"Aren't you going to get dressed?"

"Nah, I think this will be more fun to watch."

Amber was right; it was more fun to watch a busty anthro-leopard jog in the nude. Her plump, furry breasts bounced with each step. Her bottom looked even better in motion than it had when she was still. Her hypnotically sexy figure had my cock growing stiff again, even though I was much too tired for more sex.

After about two dozen laps, Amber came back to the bleachers. She took a sip from her water bottle, and then poured the rest on her face and breasts. Her wet fur clung to her skin, slicked down by the distilled water. Then, she picked up her discarded clothes from the ground and stuffed them into her gym bag.

"Don't tell me you intend to walk home like that. Someone is bound to see you."

"Nah, I've got a better idea."

She removed a dog collar and a leash from her bag and handed them to me. I gave her a strange look, but then she transformed. The humanoid leopard form disappeared in a white light. Her silhouette changed form, from biped to quadruped. When the light faded, an Australian shepherd dog stood in front of me. She had a beautiful merle coat and the same breathtaking blue eyes as ever.

"You want me to walk you home like a dog? Isn't that a little demeaning?"

"Oh, don't be silly. I've always wanted to try this, I just couldn't think of a good way to ask."

"How about you turn into a horse instead?"

"Maybe next time, I didn't bring a saddle."

"I could ride bareback." The double-entendre was not lost on either of us.

"We'll do some cowboy fantasy some day, I promise. For now, I want to be your dog. Walk me home like this, and I'll show you a trick I know. It involves peanut butter."

I grinned. "You're going to kill me."

She laughed. "Don't be silly! If I literally sexed you to death, who would warm my bed at night? I might not leave you conscious, but I'll certainly keep you alive."

Still grinning, I put the collar around her neck and buckled it. I clipped the leash on, and then stood up. My legs still ached, but

Amber was content to walk slowly. She stayed by my side, looking the part of an implausibly well-behaved dog. The leash was, at best, a token gesture to comply with the leash law. She clearly had no intention of running ahead or falling behind.

That night, she kept her word. She did coax a few more sessions out of me. When I was really just too tired to go on, she stopped. She retained her dog form even after the sex. She was still an Australian shepherd when we went to bed. She usually turned back into a human for cuddling, so getting to snuggle with her as a dog was quite a treat.

From there, our relationship continued to blossom. Her shapeshifting powers allowed her to fulfill my every sexual fantasy, no matter how absurd. In return, I made sure she never had to sleep alone.

11 PRISONER OF LUST

The ruins south of Matsu had long been a favorite hangout for bandits and smugglers. Without a regular guard patrol, it was a haven for outlaws of all descriptions. Sometimes elven fugitives even hid out there. Lately, however, a more dangerous pest had come to roost. Kobolds.

Small though they were, the dog-headed humanoids were also unpredictable and violent. At no point in the history of their species had the kobolds ever invented anything. It was simply not their way, they were scavengers first and foremost. They were often thieves, as well. Their most advanced technology was whatever they could take from the other species populating whatever area they decided to nest in.

Kobolds were not particularly smart or tactical creatures, but it was a mistake to underestimate them. Though uncultured and savage, they were also intelligent—at least as much so as those wretched elves. They were excellent at hiding and fought in swarms. They would flee if they couldn't severely outnumber their larger opponents. When a pack of kobolds stood and fought, it meant that dozens of their brethren would soon leap out and join the fray.

Clearing out a nest of kobolds was not a task for city guards; too many good men had been lost in learning that lesson. A platoon of experienced, well-armed soldiers would have to be dispatched to clear them out.

As a scout for the goblin army, I was sent in advance to spy on the kobolds. I was to report back with information on their numbers, their equipment, any modifications they may have made to the ruins, and any plans they might be devising. My superiors had floated the idea that a more intelligent creature, such as a human, an elf, or even one of our own people, might be organizing and leading the creatures. Kobolds with leadership - a truly chilling thought.

Fortunately, my observations had so far revealed no such organization or outside influence. Their weapons were rusty and damaged, some even appearing to have been picked up from the ruins themselves. Not one bit of metal between the lot of them showed signs of maintenance.

The ruins were entirely unmodified, save for a festering pit they'd dug into the dirt at the far end for their trash and waste. Though they left on several raids, sometimes multiple times a day, there was no rhyme or reason to it. They looted a village or a farm whenever they grew hungry and brought back only enough food for a meal. They had their own scouts posted and would launch an attack on any travelers that happened to pass by. Most of these travelers were elves, and some were criminals looking to claim the ruins. Goblin traders knew well to avoid these ruins, but those fool elves never seemed to learn.

Watching these creatures had taught me the secret of their numbers. They had lots and lots of sex. Even once I'd learned to tell the difference between some of the individuals, I couldn't identify any mated pairs. Each kobold would simply grab on to the nearest member of the opposite sex when the mood took them. They'd hit the ground and rut like beasts in a show of primal lust that often lasted for less than a minute; then they'd remain stuck together for a time. Some panicked when this happened and managed to pull away from each other early. But whether they pulled apart or remained together, they'd just go about their way afterward as if nothing significant had happened.

None of the kobolds wore clothes of any description. A few had scraps of armor, but none ever covered their groins or backsides. Most were simply naked all of the time; the strongest warriors had ill-fitting cuirasses. This made it very convenient for them to mate whenever the time felt right, which was about once an hour for these beasts.

Sometimes, two or three or even four males would gang up on a single female. The females seemed to actually enjoy this sort of attention. On the rare occasion that a female didn't want to be humped, she would growl and her prospective mate would find another partner without argument. Occasionally, two or three males would get together if they couldn't find a female close enough. I also observed females engaging in similar behavior when a male wasn't nearby.

I never saw a kobold show preference for its own sex, though: the same males that had willfully sodomized each other mere hours before would enthusiastically take females later. Even the pregnant females allowed themselves to be mounted and humped. They didn't seem to know or care that they were already carrying children.

Not once in my time watching these creatures was I made to observe kobolds giving birth, for which I was grateful. Large packs of young and adolescent kobolds roamed the ruins, free of adult supervision, while the grown kobolds busied themselves with other pursuits. The older children taught the young ones how to wield weapons and how to hide effectively with games that ranged from hide and seek to smacking each other with sticks. Though the adults appeared to have no part in raising and educating the children, even the smallest of them could walk and run on their own.

While observing from atop a crumbled wall, I heard a high-pitched shriek. I looked in the direction of the sound just as a female kobold smashed a chunk of dry-rotted wood into the side of my head. I hit the ground, my vision hazy. Another kobold stood nearby, a male holding a rusty knife. They spoke to each other, their language little more than a series of growls and burbles. Their voices faded as I lost consciousness.

I woke up later to a warm, wet feeling on my groin. My eyes fluttered open to see two kobold heads in my lap. My erect cock stood between their short canine muzzles, being licked from either side by their short, slim tongues. I was sitting on a stool, with my hands chained to a flimsy post. This was the first time I'd seen kobolds up close. Most of their bodies were covered in bare, brown-gray skin. Their heads, tails, hands, and feet were covered in long white fur. Their ears, faces, and digitigrade feet were very canine looking.

I wriggled in my bonds, and both of the dog monsters looked up at me suddenly. They turned their attention to each other and made some growling noises back and forth. Once they'd finished their "conversation," they turned their attention back to me.

"Why you here?" the male barked in a crude parody of the goblin language. "Why you watch us, pervert?"

"Watching you? I was just passing by, is all."

"Lies!" shrieked the female. "You watch us long time! We see you, we watch you too!"

"You have an interesting society here. I wanted to know more. Your people are quite fascinating." It was only partly untrue; I actually had developed an interest in these beasts. "Tell me, what are your names?"

"I Dekker!" the male said.

"I Kattra!" said the female. "What call you?"

"I am Kaidan."

Kattra wore an odd expression and then said my name slowly, sounding like she had a mouthful of marshmallows while she tried to pronounce it. "Kah-ay-dan."

Dekker repeated much the same process. The two of them said my name back and forth for a few minutes until they were comfortable speaking it. Then they spoke in the own language, with my name mixed in here and there and laughed. I pulled at the post behind me, finding it quite flimsy. The chains binding my hands were so loose that I knew could easily escape, just as soon as I had a chance to run.

"Why did you two bring me here? What do you want from me?"

Dekker shrieked and puffed his chest out, suddenly becoming furious. "You not get sword back, it mine now! My sword!"

"Okay, you can keep it. But why am I here?"

Both kobolds looked genuinely confused,

as though they hadn't made any plans at all. Actually, it would've been more surpising if they had. They kept glancing at my penis all throughout the discussion. After a short while, Kattra climbed up onto my lap.

"We torture you! Find out what you know!"

Dekker barked sharply. "Yes, torture!"

"I know nothing; torturing me would be an empty gesture."

"You lie!" shrieked Kattra. "You tell us where city is, how get more shiny!"

"Well, I don't know where the city is. I live in the woods. What are you going to do about it?"

Kattra gripped the base of my cock in one of her small, furry hands. She ground her tight little twat against the head, then pushed herself down on it. The first few pushes yielded no results; her narrow slit was just too small for my girth. On her fourth attempt, the kobold's pussy gave way and the head of my dick slid inside.

Dekker watched intently, stroking 3 inches of narrow, knotted, canine cock. Kattra worked herself up and down my rod slowly, her brow furrowed in concentration. She was tight enough to crush diamonds and hot enough to melt iron. Her pussy was so narrow it actually hurt, but I still found myself craving deeper penetration. With some effort, she granted my wish.

Kattra raked her claws down my chest while she bounced in my lap, grunting from the effort required to do so. She worked her way further and further down my rod, until the tip of my dick finally hit her cervix. The kobold sat bolt upright and screamed, clenching even tighter and making me wince in the process. Dekker just laughed.

"You no can take him all!"

"Shut up! Him big! Him real big!"

The kobolds argued in their primitive tongue for a time, until Kattra snarled at Dekker and returned to the task at hand. She lifted herself up a bit, then slid down again. Grunting and whimpering, she settled into a slow rhythm. Her muff fit around my cock like a second skin - I knew I wouldn't last long in her impossibly tight body.

Despite the effort riding my girth required, it seemed to be arousing Kattra as well. Her slit became increasingly wet as she rocked her hips over mine. After just a few minutes of "torture," I thrust upward with a grunt and came in her. The first squirt of goblin cum into the kobold's pussy sent her careening over the edge as well. With an ear-shattering screech, she clamped down on my poor cock like a vice and gushed musky feminine fluid all over my crotch.

Kattra rested for a time, then lifted herself off of me. She didn't unclench while sitting up though, and it felt like she was peeling my dick. To my surprise, the kobold hugged me and nuzzled my chest. The interspecies cuddle was interrupted by Dekker, who pulled Kattra off of me and onto the floor. She landed on her butt, and I could see a glob of my pearly white seed drooling out of her stretched pussy.

"You no do right! Me show you! Take him

all!" Dekker boasted.

The male kobold clambered up onto me in much the same position Kattra was in. He looked down at my thickness and frowned, now a little intimidated. After some hesitation, he spat on my big, green dick and rubbed his rump against the tip. With one hard push, he forced himself open around the tip. He clawed me in much the same way Kattra had done and worked himself further down my length. He was almost as tight as she had been and every bit as hot, but lacked the same muscle control. His bottom flexed erratically while he moved, making me squirm.

The dog-man bounced atop me, sinking my rod deeper and deeper into his ass. Finally, he came to a fully sitting position with the base of his tail against my balls. He leaned against me, panting heavily.

Kattra lifted Dekker's tail and let out a triumphant bark. "You do it! You take him all!"

"I tell you I know how do it!"

"Get off him! I want try!"

"No! Mine now! You wait!"

The kobolds exchanged snarls, but Kattra eventually backed down. Dekker took a deep breath and lifted himself up. Once only the head was inside, he sat down again, taking my entire length. He rode me fast and hard, yelping in discomfort every time he took me fully. I writhed on the stool, still sensitive from Kattra's fucking.

In time, I was bucking my hips along with Dekker's rhythm. My pelvis smacked his rump every time I filled him. The kobold suddenly stopped with my full length inside and cried out. He squeezed me tighter than ever and shuddered. Ribbons of thin, watery kobold spunk splashed all over my belly and chest. I started humping as hard as I could on the stool, making him bounce on my cock. Just seconds after his orgasm, I had mine. Dekker shivered and moaned when I came in him, while I tried not to laugh.

Before I was even done cumming, Kattra crawled up onto my thigh and punched Dekker in the face. Dekker howled and hit her back, only to be punched again. The dog people beat each other senseless atop me, sometimes hitting me with a stray elbow, until Dekker lifted up off of my cock. Kattra shoved him to the floor, then took his place.

My cock was so sensitive that the cool air actually stung a little. I felt like I was on fire. I was actually beginning to believe what they'd said about torture, but I wasn't about to tell them anything valuable.

Kattra spat on my rod and then rubbed it in her crevice. She positioned herself, then hesitated. Dekker grabbed her hips and pulled her down hard, forcing her to take the entire thing in one push. Kattra and I both cried out. The kobold woman's ass was far tighter than her pussy had been, and my oversensitivity made her clenches feel like knives.

Once she'd taken a few seconds to adjust to the girth in her butt, Kattra began to ride. Her movements were slow, jerky, and punctuated by screams. Dekker was laughing, apparently enjoying his pack mate's discomfort. Kattra growled and rode faster. Every so often, she would stop and clench hard around me. The sensation nearly brought tears to my eyes.

My head was swimming; the sensations became so overwhelming that I almost felt numb. My cock was still felt the stimulation, even if my mind couldn't process it. All too soon, I came a third time. With a buck and a loud groan, I pumped a load into Kattra's impossibly tight ass.

The kobold apparently wasn't finished with me. Her riding continued, unabated. I writhed, far too sensitive for this. Within a few seconds, she came. The kobold shuddered and splattered me with her juices, then went still.

After some rest, Kattra lifted off of my chafed tool. I quickly went soft in the absence of a warm grasp. She climbed down off of me and hugged Dekker. The two kobolds nuzzled each other, tails wagging excitedly, then turned toward me.

"You stay!" Dekker barked. "Guard outside, no let you leave!"

The two of them left the room, slamming a rust iron door behind them. I looked around, seeing several missing sections of wall. I waited for a while, to see if the kobolds actually expected me to respect the door. I could hear the dog-monsters having sex against the door every so often, but none ever came into the room.

Once I felt I'd waited long enough, I

tugged on my restraints. The stake snapped in half with a single pull. The chain became even more loose and easily slipped off. I looked around, but I couldn't find my clothes. Not wanting to face the entire kobold horde naked and unarmed, I looked through one of the gaps to ensure my path was clear. The kobolds' prison was on the far end of the ruins, I had a clear shot at escaping. With a short leap, I cleared the rubble and ran for it.

Fortunately, I met a friendly merchant who let me hitch a ride to Numano on his wolf cart, free of charge. Unfortunately, he wouldn't give me a set of clothes and I had nothing to trade. I had to face my commanding officer naked.

Field Marshal Tokine did not comment on my nudity during my report, but simply nodded while I told her what I'd learned. She seemed surprised at their numbers, but not at anything else I'd mentioned. Once my report was concluded, she stood.

"It is as I expected, then. Driving them out should be a fairly routine operation. Is there anything else?"

"Yes, field marshal. I request permission to go back to the ruins and continue observation. I have a scientific interest in the kobolds."

Tokine smiled. "You return to me, nude

and reeking of sex, and expect me to believe a lie like that?" I blushed deeply and averted my eyes, but she laughed. "Permission granted, Kaidan."

"Thank you, ma'am. I will continue to report findings of interest."

The kobolds were poised to attack me when I next entered the ruins. I told them I was a giant, green kobold who couldn't speak their language and had no tail. They accepted it without question. I tried to teach the kobolds how to speak properly. To my amazement, some even began learning. In return, they taught me sex positions I could never even have imagined.

Every now and then, I slipped away from the ruins, though I often had little of interest to report. Living with the kobolds was far from an eye-opening experience. Sometimes the things we most expect end up being entirely true. When the goblin army came, the kobolds didn't seem fazed by my betrayal. I think seeing other goblins made them realize I wasn't actually a kobold.

A good chunk of the pack escaped, as was expected. When attacking a kobold pack, you'll never get all of them. But they left, and that's the important part. There are rumors that one of the kobold packs plaguing the elven lands includes goblin-kobold hybrids among its numbers; larger, stronger, smarter kobolds able to organize and lead their brethren. I choose not to believe such rumors, and I deny having anything to do with it. Even if the stories are true, it isn't my problem. Those filthy elves can deal with it on their own.

12 WITCH HUNT

Old prejudices die hard. Though magic had long been an accepted part of life in my homeland, it wasn't ubiquitously loved. There were still many who hated and feared witches, like in olden times. These ignorant folk fortunately kept to themselves, for the most part. They secluded themselves into villages where they could ensure they lived a magic-free lifestyle. Rumor says they execute any magic user they find among their numbers.

There are also stories claiming that these magic-fearing folk sometimes capture and kill lone witches and wizards. The idea always struck me as silly. How could they get away with something like that? Surely, no witch worth her charms would let herself be taken by some mud-eating hoodlums with sticks and rocks.

The danger seemed insubstantial, until

the day I was chased by a witch hunter. He ambushed me on a path I'd walked hundreds of times before, a place in which I felt safe and confident, even outside the presence of city guards. One never expects a sword-wielding maniac in heavy plate to burst out of hiding in the middle of the forest.

My first impulse was to cast a spell on him. No matter what I tried, my magic did nothing. I fled in terror, hoping to make it to the city where the guards could help me. He was surprisingly swift in his battle armor; I wasn't able to keep much of a lead ahead of him.

The outskirts of town were a tangled mess of old streets and abandoned houses. I tried to lose him there, but I couldn't put enough distance between us to take a turn unseen. The adrenaline coursing through my veins robbed me of focus, and it was I who eventually got lost.

I came to a halt just before smashing into a wall. I'd run into a dead end. The other end of this alleyway had been bricked up at some point. I whirled around to face my attacker and bombarded him with my most powerful spells. Arcs of electricity and high-velocity ice shards danced harmlessly across his armor. He didn't so much as flinch.

"Fight me all you like, witch. I do not fear your evil powers." The armored man pointed to a simple iron bauble hanging from his neck. "I am protected from your sorcery; you'll accomplish nothing in trying to harm me."

"What do you want from me?"

"Your life. I seek to purge this world of magic's corrupt influence. I will take you to my village and you will be punished for your wickedness. When you are on the brink of death and can no longer plead for your life, you will be set aflame so that your soul may reach heaven in purity."

"You hunt witches and yet you wear an enchanted amulet? You're a bloody hypocrite!"

"A necessary precaution against your kind, Witch. People will sing songs of Aldous the Great, regardless of my methods."

"Aldous the Great? I thought you were but a myth to frighten young sorcerers!"

"And yet, here I stand before you. Have you any last words?"

"Yes ... burn in hell!"

I went for the amulet, but he caught my wrist mid-grab. A strong, steel-clad fist smashed into my face at incredible speed. I went limp, dazed by the force of his blow. I could feel warm blood trickling down my face. His armored glove had left several shallow cuts in my flesh.

While I regained my senses, Aldous bound my hands with twine. He tossed me over his shoulder like an old rug and began marching. Once the fog cleared from my head, I began wiggling and kicking. The armored hunter ignored my struggles, entirely unfazed. He carried me out of the village outskirts, back towards the woods.

"Where are you taking me?"

"I've already told you. You're going to my

village for torture and execution. You brought this on yourself by submitting to the sinful and wicked art of magic."

"Are you really any better than you perceive me to be? That necklace is magic!"

"I only wear it; I do not cast spells and bewitch others. The man who made this charm is long dead. He refused to equip all of my village's hunters and suffered for his ethics."

"Is there no way I can convince you to stop this?"

"Stop protecting the world from the wicked and evil magics? Never."

"Would nothing I say convince you to let me live, at least?"

"You could make an offer, and I would listen. I doubt you have anything I desire, though."

"Does Aldous the Great have a lady awaiting him? Perhaps the mighty hunter has spent too much time saving the world and not enough seeing that his needs are satisfied?"

He stopped in his tracks in the mud near a shallow creek, as if considering my offer. "Are you trying to seduce me, Witch?"

"I would do anything to be free. You said yourself that you do not fear magic, and I clearly cannot defeat you in a fair fight. What reason do you have to hesitate?"

"All the women of my village are old and broken. I accept your offer, Witch. Satisfy me and I will feign ignorance of your existence."

The witch hunter unceremoniously tossed

me to the ground. A sharp gasp escaped my lips as my back smacked into the cold mud. Aldous knelt before me and lifted my dress. He tore my slip, exposing my mound. With a few quick adjustments, his codpiece was removed and his organ exposed itself. I felt disgusted with myself for what I was about to do, but spotted a dagger on his belt and got an idea.

Aldous removed one of his gauntlets and stroked his limp meat to full hardness. He got on top of me and shoved himself into my dry muff without a second of hesitation. I cried out at his sudden penetration. The brute rolled his hips swiftly, bringing himself pleasure at my expense. His harsh thrusts hurt. He was only a little above average; our coupling could have actually been comfortable had he indulged me with a little foreplay. I glared up at him, angry for his lack of consideration. All I saw in return was the inhuman visage of a heavy steel helm that protected his entire face.

While the witch hunter was busy having his way with me, I discreetly dissolved the twine on my wrists with a weak acid spell. The corrosive liquid was strong enough to cut through the fibers of the rope, but gentle enough that I could avoid any major burns. Hands freed, I reached for his dagger and drew it from the sheath.

Before I could hope to take advantage of a gap in his armor, he smashed his gauntleted fist into my face again. The mud below my head cushioned the blow a little, but the impact still stunned me. Aldous took the knife from me and stuck it in the dirt. He held my wrists together in one strong hand and pinned my hands to the ground just beyond the indentation where I rest my head. His other hand snatched the dagger away from me.

"Try that again, and you will regret it." He placed the dagger against my crotch, just barely contacting my clit hood with the edge.

"I won't, I promise!"

Satisfied that his warning had been properly given, Aldous took the knife away from my tender bits and thrust it into the mud. He put his newly freed hand on the ground for support and began to thrust much harder. I cried out and struggled to get away, but he was too strong to escape from.

Tears of pain and shame streamed down my cheeks. My pussy would be upset with me for allowing such brutality, but it was worth it for my freedom. If the stories I'd heard were true, the torture inflicted upon witches was far worse than rough sex with this disgusting monster of a man. To be spared living out such nightmares, I could endure this.

I was not made to endure long, however. Aldous pushed himself into me as deeply as possible. A loud groan echoed inside his metal helm. I felt his seed spurting into my depths and sighed. It would be easy enough to prevent pregnancy with magic, but knowing he'd finished in me at all felt like a grave insult.

Even though I couldn't see his eyes

through the slits of his helmet, I still couldn't bring myself to look at this man. My cheeks burned, my pussy ached, and my tears wouldn't stop. I could learn to forgive myself later. I had all the time in the world to rationalize this away; I was going to live.

Aldous pulled his erection free of my body with a satisfied sigh. I grew very nervous when he retrieved his dagger, but he only used it to cut my dress off of me. When I was nude, he wiped the mud from his knife on a scrap of my clothing and returned it to its sheath. Then, he rolled me onto my belly.

"Please, release me. I have given you what you wanted."

"You have not. My lusts have yet to be sated; my desire still burns. You will satisfy me fully if you wish to live."

"Fine. Do as you will."

"I intend to."

The witch hunter's wicked penis did not return to my pussy, as I had expected. He instead forced his way into my bottom. A sharp scream tore itself free of my lungs, and my body reflexively pushed against the intruder. He didn't waste a single second to think of my feelings. The brute instead just humped away at my bum, burying himself in me again and again. His armor-plated hips spanked me with every brutal jab. The edges of his armor plates were curled outward and sharpened, making shallow cuts in my buttocks with every impact.

"Stop this at once; you are hurting me!"

"Don't lie to me, girl. I know you lowland women like it from behind."

"I was a virgin!"

"You are not anymore."

"Please, no more!"

To my surprise, the hunter actually did halt his movements. "Do you truly wish for me to stop? I could, but that would invalidate your end of our bargain. I wouldn't feel need to keep mine. Do you no longer desire your life, witch?"

I sobbed into the mud. The choices before me were both so very distasteful and unappealing. Continue to endure this man's perversions, or allow myself to be tortured and killed? I shuddered to think what he might do to me next, but the thought was not so chilling as what I expected would happen once we reached his village.

"I...I want to live."

"A wise choice."

The hard, fast thrusts resumed immediately. I let out a pained grunt with each slap of his armored hips against my bare bottom. He was so rough and lacking in any proper lubrication. I felt certain that my backside must be bleeding from more than his armor.

Aldous grabbed my hair and pulled my head back uncomfortably. He squeezed one of my breasts hard with his other hand, bruising my tender flesh. The palm of his gauntlet was simple chain, thankfully free of the bladed plates found elsewhere on his armor.

"Tell me you love this."

"I do not!"

"Say it!"

"I...I love this."

"Louder, like you mean it!"

"I love this!"

"What do you love, Witch?"

"I love it from behind!"

"Tell me I'm the best you've ever had!"

"You are the best, Aldous the Great!"

Satisfied, the hunter roughly shoved my face into the mud. His thrusts came even faster now, making me scream. He fortunately finished soon after. His hips pressed tight to me, digging those sharpened armor plates into my bleeding backside. His seed erupted into my bowels.

The witch hunter rested briefly, then pulled his shaft free of my thoroughly abused bottom. He replaced his codpiece and adjusted it for comfort, then put his other gauntlet on. I stood on shaky legs and tried to salvage what was left of my dress. A steel-clad hand grasped my wrist, halting me.

"Where do you think you're going?"

"You said that I could go free!"

"Do you really think Aldous the Great would knowingly allow a witch to go free?"

"I did everything you asked! You lying bastard, how dare you?"

The hunter chuckled; the wicked noise reverberated through his helm. He tossed me over his shoulder again, neglecting to bind my hands this time. His armor blades dug into my bare flesh, sharp enough to make me bleed but not long enough to present a serious threat.

I kicked and thrashed atop him, not

caring that I was scraping myself up on his armor. I felt a cold iron chain graze my fingers. With a startled gasp, I realized it was his necklace. A single, sharp tug broke the clasp and pulled it free of his neck.

Aldous threw me to the ground immediately. He drew his sword, but my magic struck faster. I poured all of the focus I could muster into a single fire spell, targeted for the inside of his armor. The hunter's sword fell to the ground and he held his hands to his helm. An agonizing scream tore through the countryside.

The intimidating armor glowed orange, and then white as the temperature inside rose drastically. Thick plumes of black smoke rolled out of every gap in his armor while he howled in agony. The vile stench of burning flesh and hair made itself known soon enough.

In just seconds, Aldous succumbed to the heat and died. His armor collapsed into the mud with a metallic cacophony. Steam rolled freely into the cool air from his white hot armor. Wisps of smoke continued to roll out of his chain mail and the openings in his helm. As much power as I'd focused into that spell, I wouldn't be surprised if only ash remained inside.

I was shaking uncontrollably. Despite my best attempts to calm my nerves, I remained high strung. Once I caught my breath, all I could do was cry. I pulled it together as much as I could and got into the creek. No matter how thoroughly I washed, I couldn't make myself feel clean inside. That vile man had tainted me; I felt I would never be clean again.

I rarely traveled alone after that day. The danger presented by mage hunters now felt a very real and present one. I never encountered another hunter after that. Whether they feared me for killing Aldous or if it was just luck, I didn't know.

I had never killed a man before, and it had some unexpected effects on me. Despite being entirely justified in my actions, I felt a pang of inexplicable regret. There were times when I saw the visor of his helm or heard his screams in the night. Startling imagery awoke me from a dead slumber every time.

It was all but impossible to trust a man for a long time. I couldn't help but to think of Aldous and his lies. In time, I managed to beak myself of that. I still couldn't feel safe around anyone wearing a full-face helmet, though. Steel masks would forever remind me of perversion and death.

The tales of Aldous the Great continued to circulate, though his story now had an ending. The legend was amended with mention of Mighty Sorceress Aveline, who called upon the wrath of the heavens themselves to exterminate that vile hunter. That was the version that made its rounds among the magic-friendly, of course. I was no doubt painted as a villain amongst the magic-fearing.

I couldn't bring myself to feel heroic, for no lack of trying. I certainly couldn't live up to the confident and quick-thinking sorceress from the tales. People came from great distances to meet me and shake my hand, but I didn't know what to say to them. I had been backed into a corner and threatened. I did what I needed to survive, nothing more.

13 NO MORE MONSTERS

"Then a pair of red-hot iron shoes was brought into the room with tongs and set before her, and she was forced to put on these and to dance in them until she could dance no longer, but fell down dead, and that was the end of her." I closed the book of classic fairy tales and kissed my daughter on the forehead. "Goodnight sweetie."

"Can I sleep in your bed tonight, mom?"

"No sweetie. You're a big girl now and you've got your own bed."

"But I'm scared of the monsters!"

"Camille, you're ten now. You're getting a little too old to believe in monsters. They're not real. You're perfectly safe."

"No, I'm not! There's a scary monster that lives under my bed, and he comes out when you leave!"

"There's nothing under your bed but dust

bunnies. I'll prove it to you."

"No, don't! He'll get you!"

I lifted myself up off of Camille's bed and got down on the floor. Looking under her bed, I could see a huge hole in the floor. Before I could wonder if some wild animal had burrowed into the house and spooked my daughter, four black tentacles emerged from the opening. They came towards me. I tried to back away, but they were too fast. I was dragged, kicking and screaming, under Camille's bed. I could hear her sobbing while the tentacles carried me through the hole in the floor.

I struggled with all my strength, but I couldn't break free. After a while, I began to wonder just how deep the pit went. Eventually, the vertical tunnel opened into a large underground chamber. Luminescent fungus coated the ceiling, casting a dim light throughout the cavern. I could feel a gentle breeze. The cavern was getting airflow from somewhere.

The tentacles placed me gently on the cave floor and then released me. I stood and turned to see where they had come from. The sight made me scream and fall flat on my ass. A hulking quadruped stood before me—a hideous mass of muscle and horn. My mind refused to make sense of what I was seeing. This thing should not exist, and yet there it was, in front of me! The tentacles folded together over its back, lying flat.

"W-what the hell are you? What do you want?!"

"You may call me Orasus, human."

"You can talk?!"

"Indeed. Why would you ask questions if you did not expect such?"

"I-I don't know. I don't even know what's happening."

"Your dwelling was built upon my skylight. The mushrooms give me light by which to see, but I do so miss the sun sometimes!"

"That house has been there for, like, fifty years. I didn't buy it that long ago!"

"Yes, the home has changed masters many times. None have been as lovely as you, however. I have watched you from afar for some time now."

"Watched me how?" The creature lifted a tentacle and brought it near my face. The pointed tip opened like a flower bud to expose an eyeball inside. "Oh, that's unsettling."

"Do not fear me. I merely wished to see you up close. You are even more beautiful in front of me. Tell me, what is your name?"

"Tanya...."

"Tanya! Oh, how it rolls off the tongue - truly befitting of such a lovely and delicate creature."

I looked at Orasus strangely. "Why did you bring me here? Why do you keep scaring my daughter?"

"Dearest Tanya, I never meant to frighten your offspring. I merely hoped that she would get your attention for me. I needed you in a position where I could drag you down without hurting you."

"You didn't answer my first question."

"Ah, quite correct. My apologies. I brought you here because I want to tell you that I think I am falling in love."

"You...what? What? That doesn't...how can..."

"Does my affection offend?"

"I'm human, and you're...I don't even know. What can you possibly see in me?"

"You are very beautiful, for one of your kind. The way you tend to your offspring is heartwarming. Your voice is pleasant. Humans are very fascinating creatures, but you are especially so."

"Well...thank you, I guess. I'm flattered really. I just don't understand how something like this could work out. We aren't exactly the same species, you know?"

"Love knows no bounds. Not of appearance, nor age, nor species. Should you shun me, I will return you to your dwelling and you shall never see me again. My only desire was to speak my heart to you, and I have done so. Before you return to the surface, may I ask a kiss from you?"

I looked at the bizarre creature's mouth with a slight grimace but hesitantly nodded. He pressed his muzzle to my lips and slithered his long, slippery tongue into my mouth. The contact made my lips tingle. Our eyes met and I felt a warm flutter somewhere inside. It had been so long since a man had shown any interest in me, let alone offered me any affection. Now this beast was telling me he loved me, and I turned him down just for looking weird.

Time came to a grinding halt. I placed my

hands on the creature's cheeks. The kiss seemed to last for all eternity, and yet it felt so very short when it ended. I gasped sharply when his lips left mine. His sad expression tugged at my heartstrings while his tentacles lifted me from the floor.

"Wait! I've changed my mind!"

"Oh?"

"I've never been kissed like that. I can feel your passion; I can tell you really love me. I can't just turn you away after being kissed like that. I'm still not sure about any of this, but I have to at least give you a chance."

"Thank you, Tanya. My old heart could not stand to be broken again. Now, I believe it is customary for those in love to consummate?"

A deep blush colored my face. "Consummate? Isn't it a little soon for that?"

"My apologies. I have not performed the act in centuries. It is...frustrating. I also realize I have been watching you but that you have not been watching me. I know you better than you know me. I am sorry for my forwardness."

I glanced at the floor, feeling a little awkward. "No, Orasus, it's okay. It's been a while for me, too. I haven't had anything between my legs that doesn't require batteries in ten years. We could fool around a little, I guess. Can your kind get humans pregnant?"

"I do not know. It is unheard of for one of my people to bed a human. I am sure we would have beautiful children, if such a thing were to occur."

"I guess we'll see. Kiss me, my dear!"

Orasus pressed his lips to mine in another tender, passionate kiss. I undressed myself from the waist down while our tongues mingled. My shorts and panties hit the cave floor. I stood there in my camisole shirt and socks, making out with a monster.

His tentacles caressed my thighs and then slid further up. One dragged itself back and forth across my slit while another slid along my buttocks. The feel of his warmth on my flesh made me squirm. I was already growing moist for his touch. I caressed his flesh with my hands, going as far as I could reach. His skin was smooth and very warm.

Our lips parted again. This time it was I who broke the kiss. I stood on the tips of my toes and craned my neck to whisper in what I assumed to be an ear, "I want you to taste me."

Orasus gently nudged me with his face. I took the hint and got comfortable on the floor—at least as comfortable as I could be on cold stone. The creature enthusiastically planted his head between my legs and shoved his tongue into me without a second of hesitation. I gasped and squeezed around his writhing oral organ. It undulated on its way inside, wriggling like a snake as it burrowed deeper and deeper. I held onto my inhuman lover's horns like handlebars.

My hips bucked softly. Orasus seemed happy to eat me out. My ex-boyfriend had always treated it like a chore. That long tongue went in far enough to tickle my cervix. The unfamiliar sensation made me shiver. The creature held himself at that depth and made the length of his prehensile tongue undulate. The steady rippling was turning me on in a way nothing ever had before.

Orasus purred while he pleasured me, an unexpected and slightly distracting sound for such a creature to make. His purring made his tongue vibrate though, which helped the surprise wear off. I writhed in utter ecstasy. Never in my life had I felt more pleasure from anything.

An intense orgasm snuck up on me out of nowhere. I pressed my crotch forward and held the creature's face tightly against my muff. With a loudly echoing scream, I splattered my juices all over my lover's face. His tongue continued to wiggle, though at a slower rate. When I managed to stop twitching, he pulled his tongue free of my pussy and licked up my juices. I shivered with every slurp.

Once Orasus was done with the teasing afterplay, I sat up and wrapped my arms around his neck in a hug. I kissed his cheek and then caught his lips again for another passionate smooch. I could taste myself on his tongue, which only turned me on more.

Soon, Orasus pulled away from me. "My dearest Tanya, I hope that you would not mind returning the favor."

"Of course, I wouldn't mind." Then, I glanced between his hind legs and caught an eyeful of penis. "Oh dear lord...."

Orasus was quite well hung. His tool had to be at least a foot long and as wide as my upper arm. The widest part of his bulbous cock head was covered in short, squirming tentacles. It was the largest, strangest dick I had ever seen in my life.

Nervously, I approached the monster penis. I knelt down in front of it and reached out to touch it. The attached tentacles moved more excitedly in response to my touch. I stroked him with both hands, feeling him throb. Lubricant dribbled out of his tip as well as at the end of all of his dick tentacles.

I extended my tongue and licked the tip of the beast's penis. His precum was salty and a little bitter, but I found his taste strangely palatable. I couldn't open my mouth wide enough to properly fellate him, so I had to settle for just suckling on the tip. I compensated with my hands by stroking all along his length. His writhing tentacles felt strange on my hands, but the slipperiness they provided allowed me to stroke my new friend swiftly without fear of chafing him.

I greedily swallowed all of the precum he could give me. The tasty fluid trickled endlessly from his gargantuan manhood. Despite my best efforts, I couldn't open my mouth wide enough to get him any further in. After accidentally scraping him with my teeth a few times, I decided to settle for sucking the tip.

My hands continued to lovingly massage his tool. The stroking grew ever swifter as his cock became increasingly wet and slick with natural lubrication. I could hear him growling above me. His thickness throbbed hard in my grasp. I knew he wasn't going to last much longer, so I ramped up my efforts to bring him to bliss that much faster.

His orgasmic roar startled me a little. A high-pressure jet of semen hit the back of my throat hard and made me gag. I pulled my lips free of his meat and coughed. Several more streams of monster cum painted my face. His cum shot out hard enough to sting, but only just slightly.

I licked my lips and gave the beast a few slow strokes. The last of his load dribbled out of his cock head. It was only just then that I noticed the semen drooling out of his tentacles, too. My tongue bathed his still-hard penis, collecting as much of the gooey treat as I could get. That massive tool twitched with each flick of my tongue.

Orasus rested for a few minutes and then stepped back from my teasing touches and licks. The black tentacles extended from his back to wrap around my arms and legs. He lifted me off of the floor and held me beneath him, facing up. He kissed my lips sweetly and then moved me towards his crotch.

I stared at the creature's massive sex organ nervously. I knew what he intended to do; I just doubted my capacity to like it. His cock head mashed against my pussy, and I immediately relaxed. This was something I needed just as much as he did. I didn't care if his girth would hurt me.

My pussy resisted penetration at first. He was just a bit too plump to slip into my narrow channel. He held me still with his tentacles and pushed hard with his hips. My labia stretched little by little, allowing him to ease his way in. Once I loosened up a little, his mighty glans surged inside. My mouth hung open for an extended scream.

Orasus held his place there for a few minutes, letting me get used to the size of his prick. His cock tentacles wriggled inside me, massaging my inner walls. The sensation helped me ignore the pain of such extreme stretching. His precum leaked out continuously, adding to my own slickness.

Once the discomfort faded a little, I gave my mate a tight clench to let him know I was ready for more. Orasus took the hint and pushed forward slowly. His mighty girth burrowed deeper into my pussy, stretching me wide all the way. I couldn't help but cry out the whole time. It almost felt like giving birth in reverse.

I let out a painful yowl when the monster's dick nudged my cervix. He obediently drew back. My lover started to hump me, slow and easy. A loud grunt escaped my lips every time he pushed into me. My pussy clenched desperately around his mammoth rod. Excess lubricant dripped from my overstretched mound with each deep thrust. The lewd, slippery sounds echoed throughout the cave.

My belly bulged out every time he pushed himself deep. The longer this went on, the less I cared about the uncomfortable stretching of my insides. The wriggling tentacles on his cock head sent amazing tingles throughout my sensitive body.

Orasus could feel me relax and picked up the pace ever so slightly. It didn't take much more for me to reach completion. My body squeezed tightly around him. I bucked and screamed, splashing his groin with my fluids.

The monster began thrusting much faster, working towards his own climax. A few swift thrusts later, he roared and came in me. The tip of his dick mashed tightly against my cervix and began forcibly ejecting thick streams of cum. His hot goo exploded directly into my womb, filling my deepest depths with creamy monster spunk. His cock tentacles came as well, filling my entire love tunnel with jism.

My bestial lover milked himself into me and then slowly pulled free. My gaping pussy hung open, allowing his seed to drool out. It felt like a hot river flowing from my snatch. I could hear the thick fluid impacting the stone floor below.

I was given time to catch my breath, then turned upside down and placed on the floor of the cave. The black tentacles guided me to sit up on my hands and knees. I took the hint and held my ass up for Orasus. He slid his slippery shaft along my sloppy snatch, then lined himself up and pressed inside.

I cried out for him—in pure pleasure this time. My pussy was thoroughly stretched and incredibly wet; there was now little discomfort to speak of. He fucked me hard and fast, rocking my entire body with each brutal thrust.

In no time, I was struck by another squirting orgasm. He pulled his girth free of my loins just as I came, eliciting a surprised gasp from me. Before I could ask what he was doing, I felt his cock slide between my ass cheeks. The thick tip nudged my anus and drooled down my crack. I trembled and hesitantly pressed back to him.

Orasus pushed forward hard. I tried to relax for him as he struggled to overcome my natural tightness. Soon enough, my ass gave way just as my pussy had done. It hurt a bit more than I'd imagined it would. My piercing scream echoed throughout the cavern.

The monster's black tentacles stroked along my nude form, caressing my breasts and thighs. One slipped into my pussy, one stroked my clit, and the other two busied themselves with my nipples. The sensations they brought helped to distract me a little.

Once I'd relaxed some, Orasus began to thrust. I yelped loudly with every buck. His writhing dick tendrils felt very strange in my rectum. The monster's cock was unbelievably slick and easily able to slide deeper into my tight bottom. He didn't stop until he reached a bend in my colon, only able to fit about half of his dick inside me.

I felt like I was going to be sick every time he went deep. It was just too much for my delicate little rump; he was tearing me apart. He sensed my discomfort and made his tentacles work harder at pleasuring me. The added stimulation helped to distract me.

Orasus kept his pace slow for a long time. His precum made each thrust come a little easier than the last, but nothing could change his incredible thickness. I wasn't aware of how close to an orgasm I actually was; it caught me entirely by surprise. I arched my back and screamed, clenching around his meaty girth and probing tentacle.

My climax helped me relax a little more. Orasus took me in faster strokes now. I still screamed a little with every jab, but it was quite a bit less painful than it had been at first. The burning pain in my lower body had eased into a dull ache. His pace increased little by little. Those mighty hips moved faster and faster.

Just as I was actually beginning to enjoy the interspecies sodomy, he finished. The feel of his spunk jetting into my colon brought me over the edge as well. My blissful scream joined his climactic roar, and the two of us shuddered in mutual ecstasy.

Once Orasus had successfully emptied his sac into me a third time, he pulled free of my rump. I gasped quietly, suddenly feeling very empty. His tentacles stopped teasing me. I hadn't realized how much he was actually supporting me with them. My bones felt like jelly; I collapsed onto the cave floor.

I rested for a while, then got up and got dressed. It was difficult to stand; my entire lower body felt sore and slightly numb. Orasus grabbed me with a tentacle and pulled me into a kiss. I suckled his tongue happily. His other tentacles caressed me, expressing the beast's affection. After a long moment, his lips separated from mine.

"Must you leave?"

"I'm sorry, Orasus. My daughter is probably worried sick. I need her to know I'm okay. I'll come back. I promise."

"Very well Tanya, I will return you to the surface. Take care, my love."

The black tentacles wrapped around me again and lifted me. They carried me through the long, vertical tunnel again. As I neared the surface, I could hear Camille crying. The tentacles took me through the hole in the floor and deposited me onto the carpet in front of Camille's bed.

I stood and glanced at my daughter. She was hiding beneath her blanket, sobbing uncontrollably. I felt guilty for staying with Orasus for as long as I had. My daughter had been up here the entire time, freaking out. I gently pulled the blanket away, causing her to scream. When she saw it was me and not a monster, she jumped out of bed to give me a tight hug.

"Mommy! I thought the monster got you!"

"It's okay, sweetie. I took care of the monster. Everything is going to be okay."

"There are no more monsters?"

I smiled. "That's right, Camille. No more monsters."

The next morning, I convinced Camille that my disappearance had just been a bad dream. That was easier said than done, however. I traded rooms with her and didn't tell her why. Now I had the bedroom with a hole in the floor—and easy access to Orasus.

I visited my monstrous lover nightly, sometimes even staying until the morning. He was sweet and polite, not to mention incredible in bed. I grew to love him just as he loved me. Our relationship flourished despite the tremendous physical differences.

As Camille grew, I couldn't help but notice that she was too shy to date. When she turned eighteen, I took her to the caves to meet Orasus. Though incredibly nervous, she submitted himself to him. He was very gentle and took her virginity as easily as possible, though you wouldn't know it from the way she shrieked.

My daughter and I shared Orasus, and he always ensured we were both satisfied. Camille grew to love him, too. He had more than enough affection and lust to go around. Neither of us needed a man in our lives; we had something better.

14 E-LOVE

Tonight was the big night. I was finally going to meet my online boyfriend. After almost two years of flirtatious chatting and cybersex, things were about to get real. It was a surprise to us both to discover we lived in the same town. We'd chosen a local diner as a meeting place.

I finished primping my long, mahogany hair and applied some makeup. Then I put on a pair of lacy red panties, a matching push-up bra, a garter belt, and some dark stockings. Next came a short black dress that showed off plenty of leg and cleavage, but was still styled to look classy. I completed the look with a pair of black pumps and a pink jacket to match my purse.

I heard the front door shut and looked out my window. My step-dad got in his car and drove away. He hadn't mentioned he'd be going anywhere tonight, but it was convenient. Now, I wouldn't have to explain where I was going. There are some things a twenty-year-old woman still doesn't want to talk about with her step-father. Meeting an Internet boyfriend is one of them.

I spent a few minutes making final adjustments in the mirror. I wanted everything to be perfect. Satisfied with my appearance, I jotted my screen name down on a nametag and stuck it to my jacket. Then, I grabbed my keys and headed downstairs.

I left the house and got in my little green hatchback. It was a short drive to the diner, but I was so excited it still felt like a long time. Once I arrived, I checked myself out in the rearview mirror to ensure everything was still as perfect as can be.

The sight of my step-dad's white sedan out front made me a little nervous, but the real shock happened when I entered the diner. Dad was standing just inside, waiting. He saw me come in the door and looked surprised. Then he glanced at my nametag and frowned. He had a nametag on too, bearing an all too familiar screen name.

"What are you doing here?" he asked. "And why are you wearing that nametag?"

"I could ask you the same questions! Was this some kind of trick to make me look stupid?"

"Me? This is all your fault!"

"How is it my fault? Couldn't you recognize me in the pictures I sent?"

"None of those pictures had your face in them and you know it!"

"Oh god, all those things we said to each other...I think I'm going to be sick."

"I'm the one who has his own step-daughter's boobs set as a wallpaper!"

"Dad, let's talk about this at home. People are staring."

We awkwardly left the diner and got back into our own cars. The drive home couldn't be long enough; I knew things were going to get weird like never before as soon as I went into the house. Dad beat me home by a few minutes, but I hesitated outside the door. I was in no way prepared for the conversation I knew was to come.

When I went in, he was on the couch with his laptop. He was deleting pictures and chat logs, all involving me. I sat down on the opposite end of the couch, unable to even look at him.

"Dad, I'm sorry it turned out like this."

"So am I. Why were you even flirting with a man twice your age over the Internet? You're twenty and beautiful - I know you can get a guy your own age in real life!"

"I met someone sweet, funny, and charming. I had genuine feelings for someone. I still kind of do."

Dad sighed. "So do I. But this is wrong. It was right before, but it's wrong now. We can't continue this now that we know."

I cast him a sideways glance. "Is love ever wrong? If we still feel something, why not let it flourish? What we had online was real, even if real life makes it feel awkward."

"Edna, incest is wrong."

"Dad, I hate that name. Call me Eddie."

"Fine, Eddie, but the fact remains that we can't continue this."

"That's not fact, that's your opinion. This has been startling, but you're still the guy I fell in love with over the Internet. It's not even really incest, because we aren't related by blood." I stood and lifted my skirt a little to give him a flash of red panty. He blushed and tried to pretend he didn't look. "I'll be in my room if you change your mind."

Later that night, I was browsing the web on my laptop in bed. I had undressed save for my bra, panties, garter belt, and stockings. A few hours had passed, and I was beginning to think my step-dad wasn't coming to see me. I still wasn't a hundred percent sure I wanted him to.

Suddenly, I received an IM message from him. "Hey."

I stared for a minute, suddenly feeling nervous, but then typed back. "Hey."

"What's going on?"

"Not a lot. Are you okay?"

"Yeah, I've been thinking about what you said."

"Oh?"

"Aren't you cold, dressed like that?"

I looked up to see Dad standing in the doorway with his own laptop. I shut my computer and answered verbally. "Maybe. Do you want to come warm me up?" Dad shut his computer as well and sat it down on my dresser. He undressed on the way to my bed until he was wearing only boxer shorts and socks. He crawled up in bed with me and kissed my lips. Any doubt vanished from my mind at that moment. Kissing him just felt right.

"I love you, Dad."

"Call me Ron. If we're going to do this, I don't want you to think of me as dad anymore."

"I love you, Ron."

"I love you too, Eddie."

We kissed again, then I pulled down his boxer shorts to expose his soft tool. My fingers curled around his length and teased him until it was fully hard. I wrapped my lips around the head and suckled softly. My tongue delicately caressed the underside of his glans.

I teased him until a bit of his precum dribbled out. After tasting him, I moved forward and took his entire seven-inch length down my throat. I massaged the base of his rod with my lips and wriggled my tongue along the bottom.

"You've done this before."

I pulled off of his length, sucking the whole way so that his head came free of my lips with an audible pop. "Of course I have. How do you think I got an A+ in AP chemistry?"

"Dirty girl."

"You're god damn right I am."

I slipped one hand down the front of my panties. The other slipped into his boxers to cup his balls. I took his manhood into my mouth again, devouring his entire length like my life depended on it. My lips, tongue, and throat all worked his sensitive rod in a well-timed pattern.

After a couple of minutes, he pushed me away. I reluctantly released his quivering member from my mouth. He pulled me into another kiss, then playfully shoved me onto my back. I spread my legs wide, letting him see the moist spot I'd made on the crotch of my panties. He pulled my underwear to the side and stuck his bare cock inside me.

I moaned, but put a hand on his chest. "Hold on, I'm not on the pill!"

"Is that a problem?"

I grinned. "If the idea of knocking your own step-daughter up doesn't bother you, I wouldn't mind having your kid."

"That's my dirty girl."

"I get it from you!"

He kissed me deeply. I suckled his tongue, then let out a hungry moan when I felt him sink more of his thick cock into my needy pussy. He took me in short, jerky thrusts. The blunt tip of his mushroom sank a little deeper into my tight pink with every push.

Once the entire length was in, he held his position for a few seconds. I savored the feeling of fullness while he appreciated my tight warmth. After a brief moment, he pulled back and began fucking me in long, smooth thrusts. I moaned for him every time he slid into me.

I wrapped my legs around his waist and dragged my nails across his back. The thrusts came faster, and my moans grew louder. Our bodies fit together so well, like we were made for each other. Every little move he made felt incredible, this was by far the best sex I'd ever had. It wasn't long before I came. My whole body tensed, my pussy clenched, my voice rose into a passionate cry of bliss.

Much to my surprise and disappointment, Ron pulled out. I released my grip on him, but before I could ask what he was doing, he rolled me onto my side. He lifted one of my legs, then slid his cock right back inside me.

His thrusts came very hard and fast now, tearing me up in the best possible way. I grabbed two fistfuls of bed sheet and held on for dear life. I tried to time my flexes for him, but he was moving too fast for me to keep up. Instead, I just relaxed and enjoyed the ride.

I couldn't stay still for any amount of effort. The swift strokes of his fantastic penis had me writhing and bucking. I could see the smug grin on his face and knew he enjoyed the effect he was having on me. I clenched tight, forcing him to thrust harder to keep up the same pace and increasing the pleasure for both of us.

It wasn't long before his incredible loving brought me to another screaming, toe-curling climax. He kept humping until I was all done, then pulled out of me. His hand caressed my thigh, and then gave me a soft pat on the rump. He lay down on his back with his arms behind his head. His cock throbbed and glistened, coated in a layer of my slick juice.

"You haven't cum yet?"

"I've got a long fuse. You can stop if you're tired."

I shook my head and then unhooked my garters. I pulled my panties down and tossed them at Ron. He caught them and brought them to his face to have a sniff. I climbed atop him and slid my glistening petals across his hard shaft. He discarded my underwear and moved his hands to my hips. I raised up and sat on his cock hard, taking the full length with a single push and a long moan. I bounced as swiftly as I could, pounding my tight pussy up and down his fat dick. His moans were like music to my ears.

Ron's hands slid up and down my sides while I rode him. After a couple of minutes, he reached up and unhooked my bra. I moved my arms when he needed me to, allowing him to free my breasts. I rest my hands on his chest and felt him caress my sensitive boobs. His fingers were just slightly rough, but his caress was gentle.

With his loving touch on my tits and the thickness in my twat, I knew I wouldn't last long. I think he sensed it too. Just when I came to the edge, he pinched and twisted my stiff nipples. I arched my back and screamed. My body shuddered atop his as I experienced yet another incredible orgasm.

I rode out my afterglow on his lap while he teased my boobs. When I was ready to go again, I lifted myself off of his shaft and turned around. I wasted no time in sinking my drooling muff down on his gleaming pole again. Reverse cowgirl had long been a favorite fantasy for me. Doing it with Ron just made it that much kinkier.

Ron slapped my ass, then squeezed and kneaded my supple cheeks. "Your butt is amazing, far sexier than your mother's ever was."

"I can't believe she left you for that waitress. She doesn't know what she's missing."

"Maybe it was a good thing. If she were still here, I never would have let our internet relationship get as far as it did."

"Good point, I guess things just have a way of working out for the best sometimes."

I rested one hand on his thigh to support myself. With the other, I played with his balls. His hands caressed, kneaded, and slapped my pert ass. All the while, I kept my hips pounding up and down his tool. I'd never done it so hard for so long before, even with my dildos I took a break between climaxes. I was starting to feel a little tender as my fourth climax grew close.

"Eddie, baby, I'm almost there!"

"Me too. Cum with me, daddy!"

"Call me Ron!"

"Cum with me, Ron!"

I bit my lip and sped up, trying to hold my own explosive orgasm back until he had his. He didn't keep me waiting long. A hard, upward thrust from him had us both crying out in bliss. Our voices melded in beautiful harmony while my pussy rippled around his throbbing cock. I could feel him cumming in me, squirt after squirt of hot seed. I clenched between his spurts and teased his balls, trying to milk him dry.

After he filled me with an impressive amount of semen, the squirting stopped. I rested on top of him for a couple of minutes, idly stroking his nuts while I sat in the reverse cowgirl position. After a little while, I slowly lifted myself from his groin. Sticky white spooge leaked out of my well-used pussy, spilling all over his softening cock and spent balls.

"Oh wow, you definitely got me pregnant."

"I'm sure we'll have a beautiful child."

We shared a laugh and cuddled up together. "I love you, Ron."

"I love you too, Eddie." He slapped my ass firmly, making me gasp. "Want to try anal in a little while, after we've had some rest?"

I wiggled my tush. "Okay, but only if you promise to be gentle."

"Of course, I'll only get rough if you beg me to."

Ron had indeed gotten me pregnant that night. Nine months later, I gave birth to a healthy baby girl. Diane was our first child, but not the last. He fathered five more with me over the years. We have always been careful to conceal the true nature of our relationship from the children. None of them ever need to know that Ron was once married to my mother.

15 GROWING DARK

The garbage bag in my hand grew increasingly heavy as I added to its contents. Picture books, stuffed animals, dolls, and other kiddie crap got snatched off of my shelves and pitched in. I had lost interest in these things quite some time ago and redecorated much of my room with dark colors and skulls. I had kept my childhood though, out of some misguided pack-rattery.

I had recently turned 19 years old, and there was no place for these little girl toys in my life. I knew that to truly enter adulthood, I had to rid myself of all of it. After gathering everything from my bookshelves, desk, and closet, I made my way to the bed.

The only thing that held me back from reaching my goal of adultohood was a stuffed husky. I was still sleeping with him every night, often cuddling him as I did. I had even given him a name - Sparky. I held him for a long time, staring into his soulless, plastic eyes. In a lot of ways, he was my best friend. It took a feat of willpower, but I reminded myself that stuffed animals are for children and added Sparky to the bag.

After double- and triple-checking for more signs of retained childhood, I hefted the bag over my shoulder and headed outside. I had already dug a fire pit earlier that day, in preparation for this. My parents would be gone for the weekend, so I had time to burn all of that junk and then bury the ashes with no one knowing I'd dug up the yard.

I sat the bag down and pulled out the first victim, a hand-carved wooden train my grandfather had given me. I hadn't touched it in years; it had just been sitting on the shelf to remind me that he died. I surrounded it with torn, crumpled pages from one of my favorite children's books and doused it all in Everclear. Then, I struck a match and set it ablaze.

I squatted down, unwilling to touch my clothes to the grass. After rummaging through the bag, I retrieved a couple of plastic dolls and tossed them into the pyre. I sipped what was left of the Everclear and watched those stuck-up polymer whores melt away. They weren't my friends. I had played with them as a child and thought they were so pretty, but now they just looked like the sadistic bitches that had picked on me all throughout high school.

The bag slowly emptied. Once I'd finished my booze, I tossed the bottle in as well. My parents didn't need to know I was drinking; it was best hidden in the lawn with everything else. With both hands free, I began tearing pages out of my old books and tossing balls of crumpled paper into the fire. Some of the book covers made the flames leap high and burn green; I wondered what they were printed on or treated with.

Once everything else was burning, I took Sparky out of the bag. I squeezed him tight in my hands and looked into his eyes again. I glanced around to make sure no one was peeping over the fence and then hugged him to my chest. I felt tears welling up in my eyes. As much as I hated to admit it, the prospect of losing him really bothered me.

With a frustrated sigh, I pitched Sparky into the flame. "Stupid dog! Making me cry..."

The warmth from the fire was making my fingers sweat a little. One of my rings, a black iron one molded to look like a demon's head, slipped off and fell into the fire as well. I tried to reach for it, but the flame was burning too hot. I jerked my hand back and winced.

"God damn it!"

I reasoned to myself that the flame couldn't possibly be hot enough to melt iron and that I could just retrieve the ring once it had cooled. That's when the small bonfire erupted into a massive pillar of searing flame. I fell back on my ass, unable to move back even as the towering inferno singed my face from the proximity. I could see a vaguely humanoid form take shape within the fire, and then the flames suddenly vanished.

The fire pit was now just a smoldering hole of scorched dirt filled with ashes. The air near the fire pit was still quite hot; the flames had raised the air temperature significantly. Standing before me was a tall, lean, anthropomorphic husky. I stood up and shakily backed away, but the dog man walked towards me.

His fur had the same pattern and coloration as Sparky's, but he looked quite real. His eyes were an unsettling, piercing blue. His pointy dog ears were curved slightly, making them look a little like horns. He wore a cold, indifferent expression as he approached. This was by far the most evil-looking dog I had ever seen in my life.

I moved away from him until my back was against a brick wall – I'd backed right up to the side of the house. He came up to me and put his furry hands against the wall on either side of me. He loomed over me, about a foot taller. His narrow muzzle came closer to my face. I turned away and shut my eyes tight.

Though I had expected to have my throat torn out, the dog man instead licked my face. His wide, wet tongue stroked across my cheek again and again. After a few wet slurps, I opened my eyes, supremely confused.

"What do you want?"

"I want to thank you, Claire."

"Thank me for what? And how do you know my name?"

"I know many things. You and I have been together for some time. When you threw my prison into the fire, I was able to free myself. Had the ring not fallen into the flame, I would still be inside."

"That ring I bought at a yard sale for a dollar? There was a dog demon in it? That's so fucking epic!"

"Yes, though I am not truly a dog. My kind is but a spirit, we cannot exist in your realm without a physical body to contain us. The ring limited my power severely. I was left to only watch the world go by. But in your fire I found a more suitable form, one I could modify to my liking."

My eyes went wide. "You possessed Sparky?"

"Don't think of it that way, Claire. I am Sparky now. I saw you cry before you put him to the flame, and I know you wanted to stay with him. I rescued him from the fire, and with my soul he lives. To thank you for destroying that accursed ring, I have become your best friend."

I could feel tears in my eyes again and gave Sparky a big, tight hug. I dug my fingers into his fur and pressed my face against his chest. "Oh Sparky, I'm so sorry I tried to burn you! I'll never cast you away again!"

Sparky held me in his strong, furry arms and stroked my back. I could feel his chest rumble when he let out a soft, pleased growl. He nuzzled the top of my head. I could feel his warm breath on my scalp. Suddenly, something brushed my thigh. I loosened my grip enough to look down, then hopped back in wide-eyed surprise. My anthropomorphized husky had sprouted a boner about a foot long!

"Sorry to have ruined the moment, but I am a lust demon. With such a pretty human squeezing me, it was hard not to get a little excited."

"You gave yourself a dick? What for?"

"Oh, I can think of a few things." He placed one of his hands atop my head and gently pushed downward.

"Whoa! What do you think you're doing?"

"Come on, we both know you've always wanted to show your best friend some appreciation. You sometimes held me to your face while you masturbated - isn't this what you were fantasizing about?"

I blushed deeply. "I don't like that you know that."

Sparky grinned. "I know lots of things...I've always been by your side."

"I don't know about this."

"I'll return the favor, I promise." He opened his mouth and let his long, canine tongue loll out. I stared at the husky's excessive pink oral organ, blushing brightly and imagining what it could do.

"All right, I'll do it."

I knelt in front of Sparky, coming face to face with his drooling red rocket. The shape was quite alien to me; there was a thick bulb at the base and then a bulging shaft that came to a pointy tip. His long, thick, red shaft extended from a bunched sheath, fuzzy and white just like his tummy. A pair of tangerine-sized nuts hung below in a fuzzy white scrotum. For a long while, I just stared at his intimidating tool. I saw him looking down at me expectantly and finally reached out to stroke it. His flesh was hot to the touch, and clear fluid dribbled out of the pointy tip while I felt him. I stroked his cock slowly with both hands, exploring it through touch. I mapped out every contour with my fingers, wondering how something so bizarrely shaped might feel inside me. Then I wondered if such a large thing would even fit.

Once I was done checking him out, I opened my mouth and tentatively wrapped my lips around his tip. I could immediately taste his salty pre-cum, and more of it dribbled out onto my tongue. After I'd gotten a taste of him, I slowly slid my mouth down his length. I took him as far as I could and gagged, then slid back. I stroked what I couldn't suck with one hand. My other hand fondled his massive balls.

I had never given a blow job before, but I intended to make the first one a good one. As my confidence grew, my head slid along his shaft faster. I sucked hard on his meat, barely able to get my lips around it but still so eager to please. Though I was careful not to, I could feel my teeth occasionally scrape the top of his shaft. Not that he seemed to care.

I could feel him touching me, stroking my raven-black hair. His hips started to buck, driving his hot pole into my mouth. I stopped bobbing and looked up at him, silently giving him the go-ahead face fuck me.

Those strong husky hands found their way to my cheeks. Sparky hunched over me and held my face in place, then began swiftly humping my mouth. I moved my hands free of his junk, just resting them on his hips and allowing them to have his way with me. I gagged a little every time his dick touched the back of my throat, but I tried to control my reflexes.

For the most part, he was respectful of my limitations. He was taking me fast, but I could tell he was trying to keep from going too deep. I swallowed his pre-cum as the seemingly endless supply leaked out. What I couldn't suck down ended up drooling over my lips and dripping from my chin.

Suddenly, he shoved nearly his entire cock into my mouth. My eyes went wide and I screamed around his thickness just as his knot pressed against my lips and his balls against my chin. My throat was burning and I felt like I was going to be sick. He continued the frantic face humping, now going deep in my throat. His fat nuts smacked my chin every time he forced me to kiss his knot.

I couldn't breathe with him going so deep. His thrusts were short and swift, not even letting me take a breath in between knot-kisses. My lungs were burning and my vision started to blur. I pushed his hips, desperately trying to get him to stop. He wouldn't budge; he didn't even slow down.

Just when I began thinking this dog dick

was going to kill me, he threw his head back and howled. I felt hot seed rushing down my throat, and he pulled himself out of my mouth mid-orgasm. His hot seed splattered onto my tongue. It had an extremely salty, slightly metallic taste. Like rusty nails and seawater. A few more squirts landed in my mouth while I was gasping for air. When I tilted my head down to spit out the foul-tasting spunk, he shot the rest of the load on my face and in my hair.

"You son of a bitch, you could have killed me!"

"Don't be silly, I wouldn't have allowed you to suffocate."

I spat again, trying to get his taste off of my tongue, then wiped my mouth on the back of my hand. "Could have fooled me."

He knelt down and reached for the hem of my pants, but I smacked his hand away. He gave me a confused look. "Don't you want your turn?"

"Not here, let's go inside."

He stood and then helped me up. We made our way indoors and back to my bedroom. It was only when I got indoors with the lights on that I noticed how much white dog spunk had dribbled all down the front of my nice, black clothes. I undressed quickly and unceremoniously. I could see his big red dick sliding out of its sheath and getting hard again as I exposed myself to him.

Once I'd gotten naked, I climbed into bed and spread my legs wide. Sparky eyed my crotch hungrily and licked his lips. The dog man crawled into bed with me and slipped his muzzle between my thighs. He sniffed me and then nuzzled my slippery pink slit. That long tongue of his slipped out and dragged across my muff in a single, firm stroke. He licked hard enough to part my folds, earning a loud moan from me. Once his tongue slid past my clit hood, he pulled back and licked me again in much the same way. He provided several more of these slow, powerful slurps.

I writhed and moaned with each lick as he was savored me like a piece of candy. A sharp gasp escaped my lips when that wide tongue wedged up inside me. He wasn't messing around - his tongue went right for my g-spot. His surprisingly dexterous appendage flicked across my sensitive spot rapidly. The back-and-forth motion had me bucking and screaming. I'd never felt anything so intensely pleasurable.

His hands slid up to caress my breasts. The warm, smooth pads at the ends of his fingers slid across my bare flesh. He pinched and twisted my nipples, adding to the already incredible stimulation.

I bit my lip and fought hard to maintain control, wanting to make this wonderful feeling last as long as I could before I came. Sparky apparently took this as a challenge and upped the ante. That unbelievable tongue of his wiggled deeper, abandoning my g-spot to instead lash across my cervix. I shuddered and squirmed at the odd sensation, but still held it in.

A sharp scream escaped my mouth when

Sparky drove his narrow muzzle up inside my pussy. I clenched around his snout, feeling the girth fill me even as his tongue continued to work my cervix. He moved his head back and forth, making love to me with his face. His whiskers tickled along my insides. That thick snout of his stretched me further than anything I'd ever taken.

It had become quite impossible to hold back. I grabbed on to his cheeks and held him in place, then shuddered my way through a screaming orgasm. I came all over his canine face, splashing my slippery love into his warm fur. After trembling through my aftershocks, I relaxed with a sigh.

A few seconds later, Sparky pinched my thigh. I realized with a start that I was still holding him in. I released his cheek-ruffs and he pulled his dripping muzzle from my snatch with a loud gasp.

"Sorry."

"That's fine, now we're even for earlier."

I smiled. "Oh yeah, I almost forgot about that."

He crawled further up the bed until one hand was on either side of me, his huge cock dragging across my leg as he moved and leaving a slime trail of pre-cum on my skin. He kissed my lips, but I couldn't tear my eyes away from that enormous doggy boner.

"I think that's enough foreplay, don't you?"

I swallowed a lump in my throat, more than a little fearful. "You'll be gentle, right?"

"At first."

"All right then, just go easy on me."

He gripped his meat and guided it to my snatch, parting my folds around his pointed tip. With a slow push, he wedged himself into me. I could feel my body stretching wide as he burrowed deeper inside. His cock wasn't quite as thick as his muzzle, but it was close. I was already good and wet for him, and his dick continued to leak pre-cum, but it still felt enormous.

His shaft probed inward, inching deeper and deeper. My belly cramped up when he went too deep for comfort, but I said nothing. I wanted to see how deep he could go. I yelped softly when his tip nudged my cervix. Looking down, I could see he'd buried about 3/4 of his shaft inside me before hitting the end of the road.

After a few seconds, he pushed harder. I cried out at the sharp, painful pressure on my cervix. He immediately stopped trying to push deeper and instead pulled back. My canine lover took me in slow, smooth strokes. It took me a little while to get used to his girth, but once I did it was quite pleasant.

He went deep enough to poke my cervix with each thrust, which was uncomfortable but not enough so for me to make him stop – the warmth, the thickness, the throbbing, those wonderful contours, and that feeling of fullness. I knew I'd never be satisfied with masturbation again.

"Faster."

Sparky obeyed my command immediately, swiveling his hips at a slightly faster speed. I ran my hands down his sides and belly. I could feel the muscles beneath his fur rippling with every movement. I began to get a sense for the raw power contained in his sexy, furry body. It made me wonder how much was his design and how much was shared by natural canines.

"Faster!"

My husky mate bucked his hips even faster, pumping that fat cock in and out of my sopping wet pussy at breakneck speed. He kissed me again, deep and passionate. I could taste myself on his lips and tongue, and I could still see droplets of my moisture clinging to his whiskers. I moved one hand to the back of his head and held him in the kiss. I gagged when his long tongue slithered down my throat, but I kept my lips pressed to his.

Sparky picked up the pace even more, growling into my mouth while he took me. I moaned for him and suckled his tongue. My hips bucked up to meet his thrusts. I wrapped my legs around his waist, dug my fingers into his fur, and held on for dear life.

Just seconds later, I broke the kiss and threw my head back with a loud moan. "Fuck me, Sparky! Fuck me hard!"

My husky mate did precisely that. He unleashed his full power, devastating my pussy with all the speed and force his powerful hips could deliver. His chisel-tip jabbed my cervix with each hard thrust, adding an exquisite pain to my pleasure. I couldn't stop screaming, lost somewhere between bliss and agony. That wonderful tongue of his stroked across my neck, painting me with dog slobber while I screamed for him.

I came soon after the power-humping started, unable to hold back even if I wanted to. He continued to destroy my pussy for just a little longer, then pushed as deep as he possibly could and cried out. His dull claws raked down my back, and spurts of hot doggie spunk shot out to soothe my aching insides. My pussy clenched and unclenched around him reflexively, milking his dick beyond my ability to control myself. Our lips met for one more kiss, and then he held me tight. I was far beyond overwhelmed at that point and quickly lost consciousness in his warm embrace.

I woke up in the middle of the night, sticky and confused. Sparky had returned to his familiar plushy form and was lying across my naked groin. I stared down at him, wondering if it had all been an unusually intense masturbatory fantasy. My pussy was sore, especially deep inside. Still unsure of exactly what happened, I grabbed Sparky to pick him up. His groin was fused to mine with a layer of dried cum, and pulling him free yanked out a few pubic hairs. I winced, and then I could swear I saw Sparky wink. Deciding to figure this all out later, I hugged my husky to my naked breasts and rolled onto my side to go back to sleep.

After that, there was never a night that I didn't go to sleep with Sparky in my bed. I never had to touch myself again; he was always there to do it for me. He would lick and fuck me until I couldn't see straight, then we'd cuddle. He always looked like a plushy again when I woke up, but I knew better. My dog and I were inseparable. No matter what anyone else said or did, I knew Sparky would always be there to make it better.

16 RIDING RED

From my early childhood onward, my mother had warned me to stay out of the woods. She told me that the forests just beyond the road were populated by a race of wolf-people and that they were a bad influence. For a long time, I didn't believe her.

It wasn't until my rebellious teenage years that I grew bold enough to disrespect mother's wishes. To my astonishment, I found that the wolf-people did exist. I conversed with them, ran with them, got high with them. I can't say for sure whether or not the wolves were a "bad influence," but they definitely helped with my stress level.

Wolven society was closer to that of humans than that of regular wolves, though far more relaxed. They lived amongst the trees, but they also built structures just beyond the dense wall of foliage that separated their world from ours. There were no roads, only paths, because the wolf-folk walk or run everywhere. They also happened to be nudists, each and every one of them. Wolves only wore clothing when leaving the woods to attempt to mingle with humans. I don't know if wolf-people live everywhere or if their population is confined to just one stretch of forest, but they're quite real here.

A week after my nineteenth birthday, I decided to visit my grandmother. She lived on the other side of the forest, and I insisted on going alone. Mother warned me again to stay out of the woods as I was leaving. I promised her I would, but promises are made to be broken.

The "safe" way was a long and winding road that led around the woods and through a nearby town. The smart way was a foot path straight through the woods. It was an hour drive or an hour walk, and the decision seemed obvious.

I got in my car and started the engine. I drove far enough that mom wouldn't be able to see my car if she happened to be looking out the window. Then, I went off the road. There was enough of a gap in the trees that I could drive a short ways into the woods, so long as I was careful. Fallen sticks crunched beneath the tires as my vehicle prowled across the uneven ground.

I stopped the car when I was far enough away that it wouldn't be easily visible from the road. I got out and locked the door. It took me a moment to recognize my surroundings. Having spent a lot of time in the woods, I could navigate fairly well after getting my bearings.

I found the foot path and started walking towards my grandmother's house. It was a beautiful day, but just a bit chilly. My red hoodie protected me from most of the cool air, but left my face exposed.

The woods were unusually quiet today. There were birds and insects making their various noises, but I usually encountered a few of the wolf-folk on my walks. They must have all been busy elsewhere.

About half-way through my walk, a wry smile crossed my face. I was close to a discreet side-path the wolf-folk used to mate. Any secluded spot in the forest was suitable for that purpose, as were their homes, but this trail was particularly popular for its abundance of wildflowers.

Hoping to catch a show, I left the main path. The wolf-folk never seemed to mind me watching. What I found wasn't a couple mating, but a lone male sating his own urges. He stood with his back against a tree. A thick, red shaft jutted from his groin. I had seen peeks of wolf dick before, but never a good look.

The wolf's furred hand moved swiftly along his knotty shaft. I could see droplets of precum fall to the ground with every stroke. The air was heavy with the scent of his feral musk. I felt like such a pervert ogling him, but I couldn't imagine why any female would deny him.

I approached slowly, mystified by the sight of erect wolf flesh. He acknowledged my presence with a glance, then was once more lost in concentration. Up close, I could see his shaft in exquisite detail. Every contour, every vein, and the wicked girth of his knot.

"Do you need some help with that?" I tried my best to sound demure, but I didn't doubt he could smell my desire.

He released his drooling prick and flashed me a toothy grin. "All yours."

I came closer and knelt before the wolf-man. His canine cock looked a lot more intimidating up close. With some hesitation, I parted my lips and took the tip of his pointed dong into my mouth. His salty precum washed over my tongue, overwhelming my senses.

I bobbed my head slowly. I took him a little further each time. The feel of his pointy prick jabbing the back of my throat made me gag. It made my eyes water, but I managed to focus on the task at hand and keep going.

Suddenly, the wolf-man placed his hands on my shoulders and gently shoved me backwards. I moved with his guidance, pulling my mouth off of his tool and lying back in the grass. A shot of precum leapt onto my cheek just as his pointed tip left my lips.

The wolf-man pulled up the front of my

skirt and shredded my panties with his claws. In an instant, he was upon me. I had grown quite moist while tasting his salty prick, but not quite enough to prepare me for his rough entry. I cried out when he thrust his drooling doggy dick into my tight muff. He began humping at breakneck speed right away.

Each savage thrust sent jolts of pain and pleasure crashing through me. He was lost in an animalistic lust frenzy. His snarls competed for volume with my shrieks. The wolf humped me like he was trying to break me. His powerful hips drove that hot love spike into my aching twat with tremendous force.

I wrapped my legs around his waist and dug my fingers into his fur. The painful pleasure had me holding on for dear life. A ground-shaking orgasm tore through me much sooner than I expected. I arched my back, screamed, and squirted into his fur.

My climax aroused the wolf-man even further. His thrusts came even more forcefully now, and his snarls grew louder to match. After a few hard slams, he drove his knot into me. The sudden stretching made me scream again.

My lupine lover took me in short, fast humps. He never pulled back far enough to dislodge his knot, just enough to jerk it around inside me. I could feel it growing a little larger with each push. Soon, it felt like a fist was bumping around inside me. Despite the pain of the excessive stretching, I came again.

I heaved a sigh of relief when the wolf-man's knot finally stopped growing. I was stretched to my very limit. Anymore and he might have just split me in half! An instant after the growth ceased, he threw his head back and howled.

Jet after jet of burning hot wolf seed coursed into me. Every squirt coaxed another moan from my lips. His fantastic sex organ pulsed in time with his ejaculation, highlighting each spurt of cum with a mighty throb. His volume was astounding. In just seconds, he'd cum more than any human man could hope to match, and he was still pumping!

My senses were overwhelmed with pleasant sensations. The feel of his warm fur between my fingers, the tingly heat of his semen inside me, and his intoxicating musk all combined to make me feel giddy. I didn't know off the top of my head how long wolf-men stayed stuck in their mates, but I was content to lie beneath him for as long as need be.

"So, what brings you to this part of the woods?" said the wolf.

I smiled. Something about the prospect of making small talk while waiting for his knot to shrink tickled me. "I was just passing through on the way to visit my grandmother. What's a handsome stud like you doing all by himself?"

"The she-wolves only ever want to breed. It's fun, but there's no passion in it. Making puppies is more important than making each other feel good."

"How was your first time with a human?"

"Third. But human girls are always fun to play with."

"I didn't know any other humans came through here."

"You're the only one I've ever seen in the forest. I leave the woods sometimes, though."

"What do you think of the human world?"

"It's beautiful, in an artificial way. Your cities are amazing. I love the sounds, the smells, and the squalor. Night time is the best. With all of those pretty lights on, it's like you have stars on the Earth. My heart will always belong to the forest, but I do enjoy my visits."

We made idle conversation for a while longer. It took about half an hour for his knot to shrink down enough that he could free himself. He pulled out very slowly, making me feel every inch of that slippery shaft. A river of thin wolf spunk flowed out of my stretched snatch.

The wolf set about cleaning up the mess he made. Quite enthusiastically, at that. His hot, wide tongue painted my sensitive pussy in strong strokes. Each lick sent sparks racing through me. The wolf-man didn't allow a drop of his own seed to go to waste. Every trickle that seeped out of me was caught by his incredible tongue.

I was disappointed when he stopped. Just in cleaning me up, he'd nearly brought me to orgasm. I was close enough to feel annoyed, but it reminded me that he really was cleaning. Showing an enviable level of flexibility, the wolf-man curled and began to lick his own cock. He slurped up my fluids from the newly hardening pink-red flesh. He was getting himself just as riled up as he got me.

By the time he was finished cleaning himself, he was hard as a rock all over again. I couldn't help but stare at his throbbing, glistening pole. As much as I wanted to make it to my grandmother's house in a timely fashion, I couldn't bear the thought of leaving both of us so excited and unsatisfied.

Before I could explore that line of thought any further, the wolf-man spoke. "I don't suppose a pretty human girl like you enjoys anal?"

I smiled. "Maybe. But you have to take it, too. And I get to go first." I pulled a strap-on out of my purse.

The wolf cocked a brow. "Do you always bring one of those when you visit your grandmother?"

"You never know when you'll run across a pretty she-wolf. Now hug that tree, and let me make you my bitch."

The wolf-man eyed me nervously, then stared at the dildo. "I don't know if I want to do this."

"Then don't. But is it fair for you to do it to me if I can't do it to you? We can just do something else, if you don't want to trade butt favors."

My furry lover hesitated for a long moment, then stood and turned his back to me. He leaned forward and put his hands on a nearby tree, then moved his tail to the side. His rump was magnificently toned. I took a moment to caress his furry ass and cup those huge balls before I stood up, myself.

I shed my skirt and hoodie, now clad in only a white t-shirt, socks, and shoes. The wolf-man looked over his shoulder at me, watching my every move. His eyes keenly followed my hands while I strapped on the dildo and applied lube to its surface. With my preparations complete, I stepped closer.

My wolfy lover let out a low whine at my approach. "Be gentle?"

"I'll think about it."

I clutched the base of the wolf's tail in one hand. With the other, I guided my dildo. I watched his pucker flex in response to my exploratory poke. I gave him a couple of prods before finally penetrating him. He gasped and whimpered, but made no move to stop me. I inched forward, easing my toy into his tight bottom.

I rolled my hips slowly, getting just a little deeper into the wolf with each push. His butt fought my silicone cock every inch of the way, but I chipped away at his resistance. Soon, the toy was all the way inside. The feel of his fur against my bare flesh sent tingles racing through me.

After a few moments of stillness, I pulled back. When only the tip of the toy remained inside, I pushed back in. The wolf-man let out a long whimper as my silicone phallus vanished beneath his tail once more. I took him in slow, deep strokes, using nearly the entire length of the toy. He was very tense, but I could feel him starting to relax.

My fingers curled around the firm flesh pole jutting out between my furry lover's legs. I squeezed his cock and felt it throb in my hand. I clenched and unclenched my fingers, massaging his meat in time with his pulse. His precum leaked freely, coating my hand in warm slipperiness.

Done teasing the wolf, I grabbed his hips in both hands and started bucking hard. He cried out and dug his claws into the tree bark. I leaned forward and bit his neck scruff. I didn't care if I got fur stuck between my teeth, I needed to make this wolf my bitch! I pounded his ass mercilessly, knowing full well he was going to do the exact same thing to me in just a few minutes.

Once I felt like I'd abused the poor fur ball enough, I slowed to a stop. I held my hips against his fuzzy butt, with the toy pressed deep inside. My hips slid back as slowly as possible. The head of my silicone dick came free of his bottom with a soft pop. I took a step back. He turned around while I was removing the strap-on, and I couldn't tear my eyes away from his quivering member.

"My turn?" said the wolf.

"Oh, it's definitely your turn. Just go easy on me at first, all right? It's been a while."

I tossed handed the wolf-man my lube, then took off my shirt and bra. I leaned on the same tree he'd been leaning on. My fingernails found the furrows in the bark where his claws had been. He approached me from behind, and stood close enough that I could feel his body heat. His long, broad tongue trailed up the back of my neck, sending shivers through my entire frame. I tilted my head, further exposing my neck to him.

The wolf embraced me, pressing his warm fur against my bare flesh. His pointy dong tickled my pucker. I gasped when he nudged the tip inside, then let out a long, low moan. He slid his full length inside with a single, slow push. Once he was buried deep inside, he reached around to fondle my naked tits. His hips slid back a bit, then began to swivel rhythmically.

My knees buckled, and my pussy drooled. Taking such a big cock from behind after so long with nothing was a little uncomfortable, but it felt too good for me to care. He definitely knew what he was doing, and it was all I could do not to melt. My grasp on the tree turned into a death grip. I no longer felt confident in my ability to remain standing. The wolf, as if sensing my difficulty, moved his furry hands to my hips. He not only helped hold me up, but pulled me back with each thrust to make me feel him even more.

The sweet, tender sodomy ended abruptly. A savage growl crept from his throat, and a scream from mine. His hips now moved at breakneck speed, stirring me like a cocktail. A furry pelvis pummeled my bare bottom, making a pleasant whump whump whump noise. His fuzzy nuts swung forward to slap my pussy.

My furry lover nibbled my neck and shoulder, just barely grazing my tender flesh with his pointy teeth. The sensation sent chills down my spine, and the idea that he could kill me on a whim added an all-new thrill to the act. Despite the burning pain in my backside, I couldn't deny the pleasure he was bringing me. All too soon, I was wracked by a ground shaking climax.

The wolf-man wasn't far behind. Before I could ask him not to, I felt him wedge his knot into my ass. The flurry of short, quick humps that followed had me screaming louder than ever. The bulb of flesh at the base of his rod grew and grew, until it was finally at full size. Tears streamed down my cheeks. I was at my very limit, and every throb made me feel like I might split in half. The sensation of seed pumping into me was as erotic as it was soothing, but wasn't enough to effectively distract me.

Wolfy licked the back of my neck for a few minutes, then wrapped his arms around me in a tight hug. He gingerly lifted me off my feet, then turned around. With the utmost caution, he sat down on the ground with his back against the tree and me sitting in his lap. I relaxed and leaned back into his fur. He caressed my chest and belly while we rested, sending little tingles of pleasure through my flesh.

"You should come with me," I said. "I have to introduce granny to my new boyfriend."

"Your granny won't mind you hooking up with a wolf?"

I laughed. "Granny is blind. She won't even notice."

"To think, just a few minutes ago we were rutting like animals without even knowing each other's names. And now I'm going to meet your family."

"Hey, what is your name, anyway?"

17 RELIEVING THE TROOPS

The peace between elves and goblins is, in the best of times, tense. Despite the best intentions of King Darrian and Queen Haruko, there still exists a great deal of mistrust. Part of it was due to cultural incompatibility. We elves favor discretion; the goblins prefer boldness. My people believe the goblins are brash and overly direct, while the goblins believe we elves are sneaky and untrustworthy.

Perplexingly, each species will insult the grooming habits of the other. As a healer with the army, I can't say the accusations of either side have any basis in truth. Goblin cleansing and preening rituals aren't all that different from elven ones.

Though our peoples had combined their armies, squads still had a tendency to segregate. It was a unit cohesion thing. It would be unwise to create mixed-species squads while prejudice still runs so strong in both cultures.

I was one of the few who welcomed peaceful cooperation—an unpopular opinion that I didn't voice often, but a heartfelt one nonetheless. Goblins were a proud and noble species with a fascinating culture. I also find goblin men to be rather attractive, though I'd never admit to such a thing.

My bodyguards were not so enlightened. They complained incessantly about the goblins. They never complained about the armor and weapons made for them by goblin smiths, though. Only empty rants about the ignorance and barbarism of a culture they knew nothing about. It was irritating, but I could tune it out. Most of the time anyway.

Today's march was a particularly bitchy one. I was tasked with offering aid to a goblin scouting party. They were camped in the foothills at the outer edge of the forest, keeping an eye on the trolls. Not every species was so open to the concept of coexistence as elves and goblins. The diminutive kobolds and gargantuan trolls seemed hell-bent on spreading chaos.

Isolated attacks by small clusters of trolls were a common irritant, but they'd become more aggressive in recent times. The goblins were keeping watch on the largest and best organized of the troll tribes. Raids were messy but rarely resulted in heavy casualties. If the trolls were feeling out our defenses for a large-scale assault, it would be a full-on war.

It was dark by the time we reached the scouting party's camp. Armored sentries were posted around the outer expanse. In the middle of the camp, five goblins sat round a campfire. They were in their off-duty uniforms, telling dirty jokes around the fire. It was standard practice to alternate guard postings. Five men stood watch; five rested. After eight hours, they'd switch.

My guards exchanged sneers with the sentries on our way into camp. While approaching the fire, I couldn't help but notice that all five of the goblins around the said fire had gone silent. They were staring at me and managed to make me feel a little nervous.

Once I was close, all five of them stood and bowed politely. My guards and I towered over them; the tallest among them was around 4'4. I curtsied and introduced myself. "I'm Corporal Mirri, a healer. I've been dispatched to offer medical assistance to your scouting party. Is anyone injured?"

"No ma'am, we don't need medical assistance," said the leader. "Sergeant Haru, pleased to meet you, Corporal. My men and I are perfectly healthy, though we do have some other needs you could tend to." The goblins all laughed.

One of my guards took a step forward and held up a gauntlet-clad hand threateningly. "Watch your mouth, you filthy green churl! You will show elven women your respect, or so help me..."

I was quick to reprimand my underling. "Alistair, be silent! You are speaking to a superior! Do not forget that we are all on the same army now."

Haru chipped in as well. "Better listen to what the Corporal says, boy. Assaulting a sergeant means a public flogging where you elves come from, doesn't it?"

Another of my guards, Firon, spoke up. "It would be worth it to teach you some manners."

"Is that right, elf? You boys want to tussle?"

I stepped in between my guards and the goblin scouts. "Enough! We're on the same side!"

"Well said, Corporal. Your men can borrow some of our tents for the night, unless they'd prefer to sleep on the cold ground."

"Thank you, Sergeant." I turned to face my guards. "You are dismissed for the evening." They stood around for a few minutes, nervously eyeing me, and then dispersed. I looked back at Haru. "Now, what were you saying about other needs?"

Haru snorted. "It was a joke, Corporal. Unless you're serious. It's been a few months now since any of us here have even seen a woman."

One of the goblins by the fire spoke. "It'd be great if they'd send a few nice goblin women our way, but an elf is fine too."

Haru glared at his underling and then smiled at me. "I certainly couldn't order you to do anything like that, at least not in good conscience. We're all a little pent-up, though. Just, you know, something to think about."

I blushed softly. It wasn't like I hadn't thought about bedding a goblin or two. I certainly hadn't thought about bedding five men of any species at the same time. I assumed they'd have to take turns. Hesitantly, I undressed. The goblins watched excitedly as I removed my uniform and light armor. They soon removed their clothes as well, baring their green skin in its entirety.

The sight of my naked tan flesh excited them. I stroked my modest breasts and watched their cocks harden in response. They were all about five inches long at full stiffness, just a bit shorter than an elven man. Though they were also very thick, their cocks had to be a full two inches across! They also lacked the spikes of an elven penis. I had always found barbs to be intimidating and had yet to offer myself to men of my own species because of it. Seeing a goblin penis for the first time made me realize I'd been courted by the wrong species all along.

The goblin men approached me and began touching me. Their small, strong hands went everywhere. Caressing, kneading, pinching, fingering. I couldn't tell who was touching what, and I didn't care. My body trembled, and I could feel moisture trickling down my thigh in no time. When they added their tongues to the mix, it was almost too much.

One goblin licked my pussy; another licked my ass. My hips rocked back and forth in between them. Green hands stroked, groped, squeezed, and slapped me. Their touch seemed to be everywhere at once. I was so turned on that I felt as though my entire body were on fire.

After getting me nicely worked up, the goblins all pulled away at once. Sergeant Haru lay on the ground, resting his hands behind his head. His erection stood proudly from his groin, twitching and throbbing. I accepted his invitation readily.

With a knee on each side of Haru's hips, I ground my moist slit across his hard shaft. His broad tip nudged my petals open, and I enthusiastically slid myself down onto him. His length fit nicely in my snatch. There was some mild discomfort from being stretched so wide, but nothing I couldn't deal with.

I rode the thick goblin cock slowly. The others moved in to get at me as well. One knelt behind me and spat on his shaft, then pressed it between my ass cheeks. The saliva on my anus offered some lubrication already. I cried out softly when he penetrated me. I'd never had more than a finger there; it hurt and felt good at the same time. He pressed his way deep inside just as I lifted off of the sergeant's cock, then slid back while I lowered myself again.

Another spat onto my cleavage and pressed his throbbing tool between my tits.

His hands gripped my small breasts tightly and squished them together around his cock. They were just barely large enough to be suitable for such an act, and they likely weren't the best set for it. He seemed happy enough, though. His hips moved fast, vigorously pumping his thickness back and forth between my sensitive breasts.

The last two scouts stood on either side of me, watching the show and jacking off. I batted their hands away and replaced them with mine. I could feel every exquisite detail of their smooth green penises throbbing against my palms and fingers. I stroked their shafts swiftly and teased their cock heads with my thumbs.

The combined effect was incredibly arousing; my muff drooled on Haru's crotch while I bounced in his lap. My hips rolled faster as I grew ever more excited. The goblin sodomizing me kept up perfectly. Having a fat cock in each hole made both entrances feel even tighter. The guy making use of my breasts pinched and twisted my nipples, sending tingles up and down my spine. He touched me with just the right amount of roughness. I could tell he'd handled a pair of tits before.

The five of them intermittently grunted. The sound mingled with my soft moans. It sounded so right, an elven woman moaning and goblin men grunting. The contrast and raw sensuality of it all only further stoked the fires of passion. My body trembled. I wouldn't be able to take much more of this.

The impending climax hit me like a

stonewall. I threw my head aback and cried out. My body shook, my holes clenched, and my pussy squirted. The goblins all stopped moving. They gave me a few seconds to clench and catch my breath and then resumed the delightful group sex. I returned to my duties as well, stroking and riding.

The goblin in my ass didn't last much longer. His thrusts suddenly became very fast. Within a few seconds, he buried himself deep and yowled. A load of hot spunk erupted into my bowels. He milked himself into me and then slowly withdrew his softening tool. He sat down nearby, content to just watch for a time. In the light of the campfire, I could see a goofy, satisfied smile on his face.

The male making use of my breasts was the next to blow. He cried out like his friend had, then shot a sticky wad onto the underside of my chin. He pulled away and used one hand to aim his spurting prick. Several more streams of hot goblin love jetted out, painting my tits with his pent-up lust. The sticky cum clung to my smooth tits and hung from my sensitive nipples.

The sensation of semen on my breasts was more intensely arousing than I had anticipated. I came around Haru's cock again. His climax came just a second later. The goblin sergeant's sharp grunt melded with my soft scream. His girth pulsed within me, filling my dainty elven cunt with potent goblin goo.

The men in my hands came midway through my orgasm. Their seed shot all over my arms, neck, face, and hair. I didn't know if goblins naturally came this much or if these poor men were just that pent-up, but I felt good about giving them such a much-needed release.

I dismounted Haru and got on all fours. I looked back at the goblins and slapped my rump. My invitation was very eagerly accepted. I had a dick in my ass within seconds. I hadn't meant for the gesture to be perceived as a specific request for anal, but I wasn't about to complain. He fucked me hard and fast, using only spit and cum for lube. It hurt a little, but I rather liked this sort of pain.

When one guy came in my ass, another took his place. The five of them took turns in sodomizing me for the better part of two hours. I came many times. Each load of goblin spunk in my bottom made me appreciate anal sex a little bit more. It didn't take long for my bum to get sore, but I was too excited to care.

When the last of them was too tired to keep fucking and they'd all retired to bed, I snuck away to bathe in a nearby creek. The water was uncomfortably cold, but I dreaded the thought of waking up crusty. After my bath, I returned to camp for some well-deserved rest.

In the morning, I was approached by the

five goblins who had been on sentry duty last night. They wanted release too, and I was happy to oblige. Fortunately for me, none of these five were ass men. My sore bottom got a rest. They ravished my pussy and filled me with their sticky delight.

I couldn't keep track of how many climaxes I had. Their thick, smooth cocks filled my loins with such bliss. When one man creamed me, he moved aside for one of his friends to have another turn. They kept going until their lusts were fully sated, just as the others had. That I hadn't been impregnated that morning was surely a miracle.

After another bath, I got dressed and left with my guards. With both holes so thoroughly used, it was hard to walk a straight line. My underlings were disgusted with me and wouldn't talk to me more than they absolutely had to. Alistair even went so far as to get himself transferred.

I didn't care; he was a close-minded fool. I was eventually able to transfer myself. I became part of the first experimental mixed-species squad. Morale was unexpectedly high, and the others in my unit boasted of my abilities as a healer. It is, after all, a healer's duty to provide relief.

AUTHOR'S NOTE

Readers: I want to expand a few of the stories to see where the characters can be explored further. If there are any of the stories that you would like to read more about again, I'd love to hear from you!

Visit my blog at www.blaineteller.com

Join my newsletter for free exclusive previews
www.blaineteller.com/in

Follow me on Twitter at
www.twitter.com/blaineteller

Like my page on Facebook at
www.facebook.com/blaineteller

Discover my books at major ebook retailers everywhere.